T0381018

THE NEW WORLD

GARY ROBERT SMITH
AKA: ROBERT SINCLAIR

authorHOUSE®

AuthorHouse™
1663 Liberty Drive
Bloomington, IN 47403
www.authorhouse.com
Phone: 833-262-8899

Published by AuthorHouse 04/04/2025

ISBN: 979-8-8230-0948-5 (sc)
ISBN: 979-8-8230-0947-8 (e)

Library of Congress Control Number: 2023910281

Print information available on the last page.

Interior Image by Maikol Aquino from Pixabay

This book is printed on acid-free paper.

CONTENTS

DEDICATION

I dedicate this story to every Sci-Fi lover
with an intimate passion for the power of the
imagination and the resolution to accept a plausible
possibility, however outlandish it may seem.

And to my children, whom I wish I could have been and
done more for. I am so grateful that they became such
wonderful people, and I'm thankful for the diversity of
this glorious world that taught them things I couldn't.
I love you guys. You are my true legacy.

ACKNOWLEDGMENT

I want to thank my correspondence for its intriguing outline and solid structure. Working in tandem has been of immense value to me.

ABOUT THE AUTHOR

Gary has always had a passion for writing,
and being an avid Artist, Musician, and part-
time critic has fueled that passion.

Gary has developed a unique writing style. His
stories touch on science for a compelling perspective
and still allow your imagination to lead the way.

His life's knowledge stems from diverse work experiences. From blue collar to blue jeans, he has seen life through the Windshield of a long-haul truck, at the wheel of a warehouse forklift, behind the lens of a portrait camera, and finally, operating a computer design software.

After completing Community College prerequisites, he enrolled in Tech School and Technical Design.

Gary decided to write full-time after retiring from Tech Design and following his passion.

PREFACE

This story is written with the concept of plausibility coupled with the wonders of imagination. Fiction can help create the plausible if paired with the imagination. Creativity has been the driving force for many of our cultural accomplishments today.

As a species, we constantly learn and long for the answers to the unknown. Science will test theories, and theories will challenge science.

Although theories and mythology are controversial and have produced unorthodox opinions from Scientists and Clergymen alike, still, we celebrate their ideas.

To accept the wonders of the past, we must assume that ancient civilizations were a superior race.

We have always been perplexed by the enormous ruins and their meaning. The lack of tangible records doesn't explain what drove the ancients to such lunacy in needing to construct them.

Time has all but erased any records of the academic discipline that was needed to accomplish their heritage. We are left with monumental structures and sparse objects of antiquity. Hieroglyphics can help decipher some of the past, but even with that, we can only speculate before that.

Following the hypothesis that history repeats itself, we search for clues, hoping to find answers.

Conveniently, thanks to science fiction, we can travel back in time and look for ourselves. With imagination and plausibility, we can see how it might have been so many years ago. It's all we have now.

So, let this sci-fi toil with your imagination, allow it to pair with plausibility, and see what you might find.

To quote the famous Serenity prayer, written by the great Theologian-philosopher Reinhold Niebuhr:

"*God grant me the serenity to accept the things we cannot change, the courage to change the things we can, and the wisdom to know the difference.*"

CHAPTER 1

A NEW LIFE

On a beautiful landscape with the sun cresting the Horizon, the warmth of the desert brought a mirage, harboring the welcoming visions of an oasis of green, with overhanging palm trees shading the pools of glistening fresh water. Standing on top of an abandoned hunter's mud hut, looking across the flat expanding sands of home, two boys watched the heat rising, as it bent the light, making it look as if the world was dancing to its silence. Darius jumped to the ground and rolled. The season was slowly evoking its dominance.

"It's getting hot, let's find shade," Darius complained to his best friend.

At 13, just beginning their age of defiance, Darius and Settie were already two independent young boys. Convinced they knew better than any elder, coupled with their insurance of camaraderie, they didn't always follow the precautionary rules set forth. Given Guard Duty. (Watchful eyes) and expected to keep the area surrounding their encampment informed of any scavaging trespassers, or evil intending wanders, that might be desperate enough to threaten their peaceful lifestyle. But as it turned out, exploring was so much more fun.

Most of the elders humored them since it kept them busy and helped burn off that youthful energy. It also gave them a vital role within the clan, which was crucial to a young man at that age. Not mature enough to go to war, yet too old for the playground.

Darius was an only child, often left to himself. His parents were separated and felt hurtful towards each other. From this, he learned that real love is not that real. It can evade without warning. His father took the separation hard.

Darius's time spent with Mother was always casual and full of chores. His father would question him about his mother's new lifestyle. He felt obligated to always reassure Darius how much he still loved her.

Darius vowed he would never experience his father's anguish. He would condition himself with isolation for days sometimes, in case love ever rejected him too.

Settie related well to his friend. He knew that the separation was hard on him so they made a pack of friendship forever. They had both agreed, on the one thing that was a top priority. On every excursion, they found themselves lakeside in the day's afterglow of the approaching evening, hoping to see a bather, and getting lucky more often than not, since the clan's females were more definitive on cleanliness than the men. It dominated the conversation for the remainder of the ride home. It felt like they were the first ones in history to discover the beauty of a woman. It would be their little secret.

For the first time, Darius started feeling Love despite his broken family. It drove him closer to God and he liked that. He would exclaim to his friend.

"A woman is God's Gift."

His Father Philippe, had taken a position at a village across the valley and didn't see his son sometimes for weeks. Setti knew that his friend's constant attention was Darius' way of filling a void in his life, and he was more than willing to accommodate him. Darius and Setti had first met at the clan's initial banquet staged to celebrate the season's first sustainable harvest. In a time when camaraderie and companionship were necessary to survive in the world. In a time of uncertainty, confusion, and ignorance. In the time of the great rebirth.

The boys were 9 then, with energy to spare. The excitement of the banquet brought euphoria, especially since it united both Darius's parents, at least for a while. The following season, life had more opportunities for the boys. With the restraints loosened on their liberties, the world had more to offer. Their inheritance of horses made the world around them seem smaller, and opened the boundaries of childhood. Tending their animals was a chore they both welcomed, creating a tight bond with their horse. It made exploring much easier and offered other intriguing aspects to their daily routine. It also gave them more free time to appreciate life.

"Ugh, I hate this place," Darius complained to Setti, sounding genuinely irritated.

"Oh, come on. It's not as bad as it used to be," Setti responded, trying to comfort his friend.

"How would you know that?" Darius snapped at him.

"Just because," Setti protested, pushing him and sprinting off, racing to the top of the hill.

At the summit, they got a clear look at the settlement below.

Bathed in the sunlight, the two settled down, lying on their backs to watch the clouds chasing each other in the sky, while their horses grazed on a nearby patch of grass. Setti thought about what Darius said. He too, felt the same. He shared the feeling something wasn't right about the place. The fallen trees, the destruction all around with no explanation. It looked so much like the scene of a war, but so far, all they had were their own perceptions. The elders were no help, commanding them to stay clear of the ruins, saying it was only for the Gods to know.

Darius, the more inquisitive of the two, had many times been reprimanded for his curiosity on the matter. Always asking questions yet getting no answers was frustrating. When Setti first suggested they start investigating on their own, they immediately started planning their adventures, and Setti knew just where he wanted to start looking. Their first finding was the remains of old half-buried statues with faces that looked intentionally disfigured. This sparked their enthusiasm and eagerly drove them to know more. One of their expeditions yielded broken-off pieces of a green woman holding a bow and an arrow. Another was a man with a beard, stroking the mane of his horse suggesting the elegance and sophistication of a long-gone era. They hit gold right away, Darius would exclaim! After that, they were hooked. Both boys started collecting small souvenirs. Jewelry, arrowheads, belt buckles, golden beads, and even a golden ankh. At the end of the day, they would tally up their finds, and then argue over who had the most valuable objects.

"Look what I got," Setti said, holding up a shiny object
"Looks amazing, can I see it?"
It's mine."

Darius reached for it as Setti slapped his hand away. Getting up to run, Darius grabbed his leg causing Setti to tripp dropping his collection. Both boys scurried toretrieve the ankh which fell just out of reach. They continued a playful yet sinister tumble, both hands gripping each other in selfish anger, finally realizing their actions, exhaustion took over and they both broke into laughter. Darius handed the ankh to Setti. But seeing his disappointment in his friend, he hands it back and says,

"Look at the design."

"It looks like a script," Darius commented.

"I know, but what?

As Setti retrieved the scattered objects, Darius examined the Ankh.

New excursions brought new treasures. Some collectibles, some not. Doubling up on trinkets, as the Setti called them, they got complacent. Much of the day, was spent at the lake where the scenery was better and the breeze was cooling.

One day, Coincidentally, and somewhat by accident, they ended up crossing over into an entirely New World.

A landscape, sheltering remains of buildings of grandeur, hinting at the presence of architectural prowess.

Magnificent structures built out of stones of different shapes stood out among the debris, giving them a glimpse into how truly advanced the long-gone society had been. Their imaginations went wild.

Who were they?

Why were these structures in such bad condition? Where did the builders go, and why were they left behind?

The elders weren't asking why the planet was damaged so catastrophically. Instead, they were denying any responsibility for it.

"What were they hiding?"Darius would say, with a hint of frustration in his voice.

"You're assuming they know?" Setti replied.

"It's just really hard when we have to keep our discovery to ourselves."

"Well, until we can give it meaning, we can't be blabbing it. They would label us trouble."

"That's unfair Setti."

"True, there may be something they are not telling us, … but it also may be for our own good."

"Now you sound like an elder."

"Where's the harm in having more knowledge?" Darius asked.

"Depends on who's ears it falls on.

Suddenly, lying in plain sight with the sun glancing off its polished surface, Darius spotted an attractive metal plate. Closer examination showed tiny engravings along the edges.

"What's that?" Setti asked."

"Your guess is as good as mine. Must be a different language," Darius replied. "I think Aster might be able to tell us about this!"

"Ok but watch the sun. I wanna be home before dusk."

"No worries."

"He's a talker. We could be there all night."

From their current starting point, getting to Aster's place was a bit more challenging than coming from the castle. The forest tended to confuse and turn one around.

Setti reluctantly followed, snapping tree limbs, at every conjunction, of the winding maze, in case the visit lasted into the night. They meandered along until a small adobe hut appeared, nestled in a cove just off the trail.

"*Unless one had marked the way in, it would be hard to find the way back out at night, even with a full moon,*" Setti commented priding himself.

"You worry too much Setti. Stop breaking branches. We'll just follow the trail to the castle on our way home. That's a straight shot."

"Where did you find this?" Aster asked.

"Close to the fields," Settii replied. "It caught my eye as the sun glanced off it."

"Can you read it?" Darius chimed in.

"It's a script that was long gone," he replied. "But one that I'm still familiar with."

Sighing, he invited the boys in. "take a seat," he said, motioning for them to sit. As he handed them clay mugs of tea, he told the boys where the plate came from and what the writing meant.

Listening to the older man's reminiscing about the ancient past was a lot for them.

Once the older man stopped talking, both boys sat still, stunned at what they had just heard. The tea in their hands was cold, and their heads were spinning with the newly found knowledge.

The broken derelict remains of the buildings and structures scattered around them that the older man spoke of, were starting to make some sence. Items that littered the landscape took on a more significant meaning.

While the older man spoke of the past wars, Settii noticed a broken brick in the wall behind him. Covered with thick creepers and roots of a large old tree torn right through the middle, Time seemed to have gained more authority on the planet than its current inhabitants. It was slowly taking back man's achievements of a civilization long forgotten.

Once the older man finished talking, he momentarily sat silently with a concerned stare.

"Umm, can you please tell us more?" Settii asked.

Darius followed Settii's lead and requested the old man to "Please tell more."

"It could be harmful to know too much," the old man replied.

The man's eyes were fearful and teary. There were parts of his story that he was unwilling to share. The older man himself hadn't been born on the planet. He was the descendant of a Hermetite family exiled from their home planet for a political scandal long ago, when Aster was young and innocent. His sparse darker memories of the era paused his train of thought for a moment.

"Sir, please tell us more. You're our only source. The elders in the village refused to talk about it."

"Listen, boys," he said. "I have seen the worst, heard the worst, and some things can be dangerous to even speak of. I'm a bit superstitious, and if I speak of too much evil, I fear the evil will return. But believe me when I say, I believe the tragedy is not done with this world yet. It will strike again. It's only a matter of time before history repeats itself. What you see today are the remains of a battle of epic proportions. People like you were living peacefully until the destruction started. Yes, your people were also one of the architects of your destruction. Gradually, some people took to the sky, some went under the rocks, and the rest were victims of disorder, famine, and disease. Once their systems fell apart, chaos followed, and even the thought of peace became a myth, and that's all I'll say about that."

The Boys listened to the older man attentively, relieved to know they had found someone who had lived during some of the lost periods.

"My bloodline is not of this planet. My family ended up here under protest, and this planet eventually became our home. There was evidence of war when we first arrived. I can see that the planet is now recuperating. I see you both as an example of this," he said slowly, his voice akin to gravel under someone's shoes.

"Did you see any destruction happening?" Darius asked.

"Whatever happened during the wars, I know from stories the elders told me, and the records they left behind. It's easier to remember the time when things started to get better, trees started to grow, and women started giving birth again. This planet has a lot of secrets, and not all are pleasant. Are you sure you want to know more?" Aster asked, his serious expression turning even grimmer.

"Please," Settii pleaded.

"Some people survived, and so many didn't, yet nature continued to act as it is supposed to," Aster replied, sounding somewhat cynical.

The boys looked at each other, their faces apprehensive, which soon gave way to curiosity. Aster continued.

"To make a disastrous story a little less disastrous, it has been centuries since the last flying machine left this land because those leaving, felt it was irreparable." He grinned slightly. "The planet is now recuperating and has at last found life. As I said before, nothing more represents new life than children."

Surprisingly, Aster sounded genuinely happy.

"flying?" asked Darius. "Like a bird?"

"Yes," Aster clarified with a laugh. "You must have seen them yourself. They circle like buzzards over the planes."

"We stay pretty close to the village. Its required."

"Well, lets not say (close)" Settii said. "We try at least."

"We can speak of that later!" Aster said

"Well, at least tell us more about what life was like for you!" exclaimed Settii.

"Alright, alright, take it easy, the two of you. It's a long story, and if you're interested." Aster continued. "The first thing you need to understand is there are three major groups of people involved; the Earthlings – that's you guys, the visitors – that's me and my people; and the Jackles– the group that I feel is to be blamed the most for the devastation."

As Aster went on, the following story had the two boys awestruck. When Aster noticed the bewildered look the boys were both exhibiting, he thought it best to stop.

"Alright then, I've talked enough," Aster said. "You two best be going now because it will be dark soon."

The boys realized that they had been so mesmerized by stories, they had lost track of time.

"We can talk later." Aster said.

Waving their goodbyes, the two mounted their horses and headed toward the settlement in silence, lost in thought. The two contemplated what the older man had told them. They thought about what he had said about life, before the calamities that shook their world, about the tall buildings and the flying machines that flew across the planes.

They thought about the devices they used to light the landscape at night without fire and how they looked like little stars in the sky when seen from a distance from the hillside. The kind of information that needed more clarification.

Settii finally broke the silence, "Do you think the old man is telling the truth … I mean, sure, the ruins and the things help make his words valid, but what if he just made all that up? What if he's been alone so long that he's lost his mind and just created theories to deal with his isolation?"

Darius replied, "Lots of his story made sense, and lots of it was hard to believe, like the bit about space pirates, but I can tell you this much. Old man Aster isn't crazy. I've heard the King often consults with him. He is a trusted resource."

The settlement the boys called home was a far cry from the urban spaces described by Aster. The influence people had over their surroundings had reduced drastically if what he was saying was true.

As the boys neared their home, they looked back to see the sun had just begun to dip beneath the horizon.

"Right on time, huh?" said Settii.

They climbed to the top of the last hill to view their

clan's settlement; the tents, mud houses, pack horses, and neighbors came into sight. They rushed down the hill, urging their horses faster, and only slowed their pace when they heard someone call from behind them.

"Halt!!" said a gruff voice.

The two stopped dead in their tracks and turned around right away. It was Big Bakaii riding up on his horse. Bakaii was a behemoth of a man who stood at seven feet and two inches and wielded a longbow and arrow when on horseback with a battle axe strapped on his back. Marked with scars inflicted by both man and beast – neither victorious, the most prominent running across the right side of his face down to his jaw.

"Oh… it's just you two runts," he said, almost disappointed. "Cutting it a bit close to sundown, aren't ya boys?"

"We're okay. We just took a little longer out there because we had some questions for the old man by the ruins," Settii replied.

"Oops, you shouldn't have said that." His partner in crime remarked.

"You mean old Compass?"

"Compass? That's his name?" replied Darius

"Astro Compass. Nicknamed because of his innate ability to always find his way home," Bakaii responded.

"His name is Aster," Settii barked. " And he's no compass."

"Suite yourself."

Bakaii grunted, realizing the boys were getting older, and slowly losing their vulnerability. He trotted along with them leading them toward the trench that guarded the inner part of the settlement.

"But why were you two there?" He asked. "What would we have done if there was any danger around?"

The boys looked at each other and then back at the old man with the sarcastic expression, OH YEAH,, SORRY. Bakaii knew as well as anyone, that there had been no chaos around the village in years.

Giving guard duties to the boys was not as severe as the elders made them out to be, but it helped give youngsters an identity and teach them responsibility.

"Let us off, just this once, Bakaii," Dariuas pleaded. He looked at the old man's horse with a snarl in his upper lip quickly curbing the conversation, he asked about Bakaii's horse.

"What are you looking at, brat?" The old man asked in a joking manner.

"What kind of a name is Diogenesis?" Darius quickly replied. "It sounds ancient."

"My great great great grandma knew a guy who went by the name Diagenesis. The story is that he was the God of Rocks. Or maybe he just pretended to be one. Either way, he lived in a box sometimes, not one of our tents. And he did not live by our customs. He was a hardened outlaw, as hard as a rock, I can tell you," Bakaii smugly replied. "As he patted the horse's neck. "Just like my wild mare here."

"That's … amusing," Settii said,

Settii was the intelligent yet slightly arrogant boy who sometimes came across with sarcasm. But he also knew that, since Bakaii's horse story was passed down through so many great-grandmothers, the story would most likely be grossly inaccurate by now if not completely bogus.

"What's amusing?" the old man asked.

"We've heard many stories today," Settii pointed out.

"Good for you," Bakaii growled, returning to his guarded self.

"Well, I'll have a story to tell your parents so they can give you a good hiding! How many times have they told you not to stay out too late? You also chose to abandon your post because you wanted to listen to the tales Old Compass had to tell!" Bakaii reprimanded them. "Seems everyone has a tale to tell these days."

The boys shrugged shoulders apologetically. The two had almost gotten away with it, but Settii had gotten them in trouble again. Suddenly, he had an idea.

"The last one through the gate is a horse dung pate!" he yelled as he urged his horse into a gallop. Darius followed suit swiftly, and the two boys laughed as Bakaii roared at them, trotting along behind them.

The three entered the settlement's inner space, welcomed by the campfires' warmth, the children's laughter, and the smell of supper in massive communal pots the women had placed in the general cooking area.

As each went their way, Settii could not help but imagine what his home would have looked like had it been a part of the Old World. Had his village even existed then? All he knew was it was there now, and it was good to be home.

CHAPTER 2

THE VISITORS

The settlement was peaceful. It stretched out over hills and mountains, slowly regaining life. After the planet's destruction, the survivors lived underground for an extended period. They survived on stored food, scarce roots, and wild berries. A select bunch of men ventured to the surface often to gather more supplies while defending against animal predators killing the more aggressive ones. Butchering and Cooking techniques were slowly adopted, and in time, their diet slowly turned to meat. It didn't take long before the labor became less for protection and more for survival.

They huddled close in winter, and fires from dry wood were one of the things they considered a luxury. After many seasons, vegetables started to grow again from the ashes. The community had expanded, and they began to emerge from their caves, realizing they could also live above the ground.

They had forgotten much of their history as more years passed in ignorance until bliss became the norm. Although the devastation around them suggested differently, no one questioned what had happened before or why – life was hard, and the focus remained on surviving the elements.

The community's population expanded in what felt like overnight, creating a need for a governing system and appointing organizational systems to address the community's needs. A justice system implemented new laws to help arbitrate and control the chaos that larger populations too often seemed to breed. Brawls from disagreements would sometimes get out of hand.

As time moved on, lifestyles got better. The older kept any talk of the devastating war away from the young. No one wanted to admit that a weaker generation had given up hope. So much of that dark history was lost, erased to the annals of time. According to the remaining descendants, it was a time of despair and desperation, and any stories told were best left alone.

King Howard was the ruler of all the territory. Under his domain came every citizen who had, un-biasedly appointed him. Even though his heritage was, in fact, royalty, his stature had not been automatically handed down through the family. His father always believed hard work and dedication were the key to success.

Before the division of the population into two small villages, each town employed a single leader responsible for overseeing all the hunters, farmers, and scouts. One of these two leaders was slated to become the King's successor. At the same time, another was chosen leader from that perspective villages and would fill his vacancy, which resulted in the celebration of the royal promotions for both. A festival like no other, provided you were still alive to attend it.

The town so liked their celebrations. They staged several through the seasons. King's-Day, thanks to his kind offerings, Harvest Day, in thanks to the miracle of seeds. A Day reserved for the loved ones who passed and remembered their heritage left behind. They were constantly gathering on Hallowed ground.

Solar eclipses were more of a mystery than a celebration, but still a similar random recurrence of the midday sun disappearing, which happened very seldom but signaled a time to convene from the fear of a war between the deities. Lasting for a short time and then returning. It wasn't a celebration of sorts, more like a ritual in honor of the angry Gods causing solace and somberness. Some would gather for weeks afterward, praying for forgiveness for their sins. Others would rejoice in the fulfillment of their God's victory that day.

King Howard was once a village leader and remained loyal to his roots. He was humble and kind, attempting to reign as justly as possible. His palace had an open-door policy for all – they could approach him anytime. Any citizen could call upon him and ask him for assistance.

Additionally, he supported the placement of a massive bell in the middle of the two cities. It was hailed as the peacekeeper. Ringing the bell would receive immediate attention or assistance from either city in the event of an alien assault, It was meant to bolster their defenses much more quickly. Like a call for help. Any prankster calling 'Wolf' would be severely reprimanded.

It also signaled general meetings for the senior advisers. There was a rotated bell ringer usually passed to a younger replacement annually. Either village had its code.

There was no incentive for taking the position, but since it had some compensation, with little participation, it often attracted the young.

Darius and Settii had often been to the palace court, and eventually, King Howard could recognize them from a distance. The elders had repeatedly complained about their inquisitiveness and curiosity but Howard welcomed it. He'd also seen them lurking around the ruins and other areas, far from their scouting posts, whenever they'd gotten the chance to sneak off.

One day, both boys were bored, standing at their scouting post near the palace. The palace itself was a restored ruin of a very old cathedral. It had a great hall, a throne room, stained glass windows, and a heavy oak wood door with iron hinges oiled to protect them from the harsh environment and ensure they remained functional.

The only downside of the magnificent piece of architecture was its location on the furthest edge of the city. It was nearer to the areas filled with wreckage deemed too dangerous to navigate, which surrounded the palace from all sides, excluding the front entrance, as a natural safeguard surrounding the building.

Darius was the one who had decided to investigate the grounds. Settii, being the more cautious one, had reluctantly followed along. Darius was a risk-taker who liked treading dangerous waters and flirting with disaster. In contrast, albeit more intelligent, Settii was always trying to curb Darius's spontaneity.

Darius was shifting the wreckage around, trying to find something interesting. At the same time, Settii sat nearby on a pile of rocks, contemplating scenarios, as he often did.

He was suddenly brought out of his reverie when he caught a glint of metal in the distance and looked up. Surprised,

"Darius!" he called out urgently, then jumped down from the pile of rocks and grabbed Darius's shoulder, dragging him behind it, ensuring both were hidden from the palace guard's sight.

"What? What?" he asked,

"Look! That's the Visitor's Captain."

"Yeah, right,"

"No, I mean it. Look at what he's wearing."

Although the Visitors weren't from Earth, they did populate a large part of it. Their motives were a mystery; even though they had generated many rumors,

Some locals thought they were evil, responsible for the Earth's downfall and rampant destruction. Many blamed the Visitors for being the ones to cause the wreckage and claimed that they would do it all again. Others believed that the Visitors wanted to live peacefully and recluse.

Even though they'd simulated the local language, they used their own language among themselves.

They had small boxes that emitted music. Most importantly, they possessed long, metallic cylindrical weapons capable of stopping a person with one blast.

If they were, in essence, a peaceful bunch, they certainly had the potential to be menacing. Settii and Darius thought the Visitors were a threat to the Earth's population.

"He's an Alien, alright," Darius whispered as he noticed what he was wearing. "But he might not be the Captain."

"It's their Captain." Darius insisted. "I saw his rendering beside the fruit stall just yesterday. Captured by that image devise they possess."

"He might just be exploring. Let's follow,"

"Stay Low!"

The boys waited to see what would happen, staying near the ground while attempting to be stealthy by darting between all the wreckage.

They watched as the captain and his small group of armed men confronted the stationed palace guards. The boys picked their way through the landscape to King Howard's Palace and suddenly realized the aliens were armed with the stick objects the boys had been taught to recognize and fear.

"We need to tell someone," Settii urged. "They're

pointing towards the palace. If they get by the guards, there could be trouble.

"Yes, but who can we tell? The hunting team has moved to the South, and that's way too far to get to them in time!" Darius said.

"Old man Aster," Settii said, his eyes brightening. "Aster would know what to do. His home isn't far away either."

Darius nodded, and the boys hastily ran towards Aster's adobe. Within minutes, they arrived and banged on the door till he opened up.

Aster looked at their frazzled expressions and was immediately concerned.

"Where's the fire, boys?" he asked. "What has occurred?"

Darius exchanged a glance with Settii, both still catching their breaths.

"They're here," Darius began.

"Who?"

"Their Visitor Captain is making his way to King Howard's Palace right now."

Aster looked shocked at the news.

"The Visitor's Captain? To Howard?" he asked.

Darius whispered, "Did I say, Captain?"

"He looked like a Captain to me."

For a minute, Aster thought and contemplated the situation. Then he hurriedly pulled his cloak from the rack and donned it.

"We must hurry, boys. I must help in any way we can."

With that, he stepped out of his ruins and made his way through the small batch of trees, left standing after the carnage, making the way to the palace. The boys were shocked at Aster's reaction. It was the first time they had seen him step out of the safety of his humble abode. Even when the elders needed help, it was an unspoken rule that if one wanted Aster's advice, one had to go to Aster to get it.

As he led them through the woods, taking the shortest route back through the forest, the boys were surprised to see how agile he was for his age; they were struggling to keep up. Aster had left so quickly that he'd forgotten the staff he usually carried, but the boys saw that the missing cane was helping him. It must be his weapon instead of his mobile assistance, Settii thought.

Soon, they stepped out of the woods, clear of the wreckage, right in front of guards, who had recognized him and quickly escorted them to the palace doors. Immediately Aster rushed in, storming in without any ceremony or decorum. The boys followed behind, feeling a bit shy and distant.

"How's he do that?" Settii asked.

"Do what?"

"The Guards must trust him."

A little confused himself, and thinking; it's all about who you know these days. A feeling of privilege that they were allowed into the King's court, if only briefly.

Darius wanted to storm in beside Aster, but his friend grabbed his arm and kept him behind thinking, that someone would need to return the news to the clan, and he preferred that they both made it home alive. "Who knows what the visitor and his entourage had in mind with this unscheduled visit," Darius whispered.

King Howard sat on his throne with an expression of surprise as Aster burst into the hall. The Captain / Visitor stood before him, and he looked equally shocked. They had been talking about something before the rude interruption. Settii thought he overheard the words "negotiation" and "camaraderie " as soon as they arrived.

"What is the meaning of this?" The Visitor exclaimed as saw Aster rushing in.

King Howard remained silent, only fixing his gaze on Aster, who walked past The Visitor, ignoring him, and climbed up to King Howard's dais and pointed down.

"Do not listen to a word that comes from the mouth of these liars. They have come over to take the throne. Their intentions are malignant. They must be removed!" Aster commanded.

Both King Howard and The strange intruder were stunned by his declaration.

"You are mistaken. We tell no lies. Our intentions are not the throne. We come in peace," Karl said.

His voice was deep, but it had a melodic tone to it. His eyes were intelligent and precise. His hair was longer, ending just below his earlobes, instead of closely cropped, as the Earthlings did. He was extremely pale and wore shoes with his toes showing.

"I know of this kind; they are not as sympathetic as he wants you to believe," Aster commanded.

"Look how he comes before you with his toes revealed

and rings in his ears. If a Visitor can show such contempt to you, King Howard, imagine what his seniors must be like. Why should we deal with those who so openly disdain our traditions? Is it because of ignorance? I think not!"

Settii nearly gasped in surprise. That was a sign of disrespect in the villages. Shoes were supposed to cover people's feet fully. It was just one of those traditions that originated and took root. Apart from that, the alien wore large ear hoops that hung from each ear, another massive sign of disrespect to the local culture. Men and women who impaled their ears were often frowned upon and expressly disliked.

"Peace!? "Aster exclaimed. "After all the wars you caused, you say you come in peace?".

"What do you mean?" The alien asked.

"You are the ones who started the End War!" Aster accused.

"We started no wars!" the alien Captain Karl thundered. Then he turned to King Howard. "Does this man speak on your behalf when he makes these accusations? Do you believe as he does, or will you listen to what I say?"

He did not look at Aster, waiting for King Howard's final decision.

"You started the war?" King Howard asked, his eyes widening.

"No ..."

"Yes! They did!" Aster exclaimed.

Captain Karl sighed and said, "No, we did not. I ask you

once again. Do you believe as he does, or will you listen to reason?"

King Howard stood up.

"I have made my decision. Aster has served me honestly and faithfully during my reign as King. I trust his word. The Aliens have given nothing to my people before, so why should I accept what you offer here?"

"We're bringing something to your people now," Captain Karl said, fighting back his anger. "All you need to do is to extend your hand and take what I offered."

"That sounds more like an order than a request. We are not beggars, and we take no charity. I will hear no more from you," King Howard said. "Begone or begoustged."

"Begousted?" Darius turned to his friend.

Surging his shoulders, "Royaly talk?" Settii said. "I think it means, (thrown out.")

He turned to his guards and motioned for them to remove the presumptuous visitors.

"We come with intentions of an alliance. We're extending a hand of friendship," Captain Karl said coldly, ignoring the approaching guards advancing quickly.

"Your demeanor does not convey it. I don't trust you or your slippery tongue!" King Howard declared. He nodded to the guards and said, "Throw them out!"

Karl did not budge as the guards advanced, so they drew their weapons, notched their bows, and aimed.

"We come in peace!" Captain Karl repeated patiently.

The guards barely faltered in their steps, immune to his words. Captain Karl's guards lifted their weapons, the deadly cylindrical shock sticks, ready to fight back, but Captain Karl raised a hand, signaling them to back down, and they lowered them.

Settii was surprised to see that. Captain Karl stood unafraid in the ruined cathedral, even with all arrows trained on him. He saw the visitor as brave because he was not looking to harm anyone, even while facing a severe adversary. However, his first impression of Captain Karl needed to be corrected.

Then Karl retreated.

"Think again!" he started to say but never got a chance to finish his sentence. The guards opened the door and shoved the visitors unceremoniously outside, where they landed on a heap on the ground. Then just as quickly, they shut the door behind them. Karl knew that with all the Kings men in place, had there been any confrontation, his men would be unlikely to make it out of the Palace doors, even with their superior weapons.

Captain Karl stood up, brushing off his clothes. He scowled, annoyed at the harsh treatment. He had the power to raze the entirety of King Howard's population and take over his lands.

Instead, he had offered peace, yet his peace offer had been brutally denied. He decided against letting this little incident go. He felt insulted and extremely slighted.

"Mark my words, Howard," he said, his voice carrying through the thick wooden doors. "One day, you will need us, and we will refuse to assist you like you refused our peace offer."

Then he turned around and made his way out of the community. As he walked, he talked to his men in his language.

"Qi common, du lat un destro....." "*We're going to make them pay for this,*" Captain Karl said.

"*Our weapons are at your disposal,*" the men reassured him.

Captain Karl walked away, fully intending to conquer Howard's lands, take them for his own, and ultimately destroy the local population. He had never been as insulted or slighted as he had been just then, and he hated the feeling.

With that, he and his guards made their way across the wrecked land, feeling more like a defeated pawn than a glorious ruler.

King Howard turned to Aster, and the two embraced.

"How fare you my friend?" he asked.

"I am well," Aster said. He smiled at King Howard. "You made the right decision."

King Howard nodded grimly.

"It is all thanks to you, my old friend," he said.

The boys looked at each other. They were glad to have been able to help, but Settii still felt something was not quite right.

"Why did the alien back down?" he said.

"I think he has alternative plans."

"I don't think that's it," Settii said. "I think he did come in peace."

"But old man Aster's decision-," Darius started to say.

"Aster has the potential to be flawed, just like Old Bakaii. I think this may have earned us an enemy," Settii said gravely.

The boys decided to leave the palace discretely. They had had enough excitement for the day and realized they had to sneak in before the scouting teams realized they had been off on another adventure.

CHAPTER 3

THE FORTRESS

Captain Karl was enraged. He had come for peace, and the King had thrown him out, much to his immense humiliation. He never expected such treatment from an inferior, unadvanced species. The whole idea irked him.

Mud covered the hem of his coat. He had avoided getting it dirty when he had picked his way toward the palace, but the inconsiderate removal had done the opposite. He groaned at seeing it, looking back at his two bodyguards. Karl was the only one to hit the ground.

"Not a word of this to anybody," he warned. "Do you understand?"

"Yes, sir," they said, in sync.

"The Earthlings have humiliated and demeaned us. I swear to you, right now, that I will take over their entire colony of peasant warriors and make them pay for this. I will make them regret the day they turned us away," Captain Karl vowed.

He started walking briskly, looking around at the marshlands, thinking about what an absolute waste it was.

He had seen how Earthlings had once initially cultivated growth on the planet's surface. They had cluttered the surface with bright, colorful homes and beautifully detailed sculptures. Huge chapels and atriums had occupied the land, but then, so had grief, disease, poverty, and hatred.

He had envisioned the local's end even before the destruction became apparent. They built things but often destroyed other, more beautiful things while making them. He had often wondered what would have happened if he had taken over their land before they had had the opportunity to ruin it.

He was not quite used to the Earth's temperature, time, air quality, ground, or gravity. Tasks he was used to accomplishing in a day seemed to take the Earthlings forever to do the same.

One day on his planet was equal to five days here. He had plans to let the locals make significant advancements, and once accomplished, he intended to treat them like lab rats and enslave them all, but recent occurrences had changed everything.

He had already summoned his ship to meet him at ground level. His ship was a massive vessel, currently in constant orbit around the Earth, keeping in place with the Earth's revolutions. At that very moment, it was hovering at the top of the tallest mountains since that had been the most accessible spot for the away scouts to use as a landmark and accessible with the land pods.

He reached his ship via the transport vehicle and pressed a button on his wrist. The Hermetites had very distinct attire. They wore tights, and a long shirt made entirely of a woven chain-like material and reached their knees. On their wrist, they wore metal bracelets. Captain Karl wore a metal brace piece on his arms with buttons on it. One to summon the ship ground level, and another to recall it to his stealth location.

Just as he pressed the button, a massive strap running across its base, which made up the ship's main entrance, unfolded into a ramp, leaving an opening for the captain and his bodyguards to enter quickly.

As soon as he stepped off the transport, the floor's surface beeped. It was wired to self-clean and sensed the marsh mud on Captain Karl's clothes. Suddenly sanitation lasers came out from behind the walls.

Karl stood still while a thin beam of white light focused on Captain Karl's clothing till the mud was gone. They worked by a simple disintegration system that used hadron collider energy to break apart dirt particles into their corresponding nitrogen and salt components.

Once the lasers had done their tasks, they retreated within the walls, and Captain Karl briskly stepped forward and let himself recline on a velvet-lined couch, then sent the ship back up with a verbal command.

"Return!" he ordered as they accelerated back into low orbit.

The ship spanned over 10,000 square feet and harbored three hundred Hermetites that had volunteered to seek out planet Earth with Captain Karl, who had boasted about its plentiful resources. All of whom were still waiting to see.

Captain Karl frustratedly settled his head in his hands, dismissing the guards.

"Those Earthlings. Those terrible, terrible Earthlings. They destroyed their planet and destroyed their race. How could anyone be that ignorant?" he said aloud. "Perhaps the Elders were right. Reaching out to the inferior species intent on self-destruction is a waste of time. Perhaps that is why the more intelligent species have never tried to ally with Earthlings in the past."

The thought of how the Earthlings' King had kicked him out brought a rage back to him. "Think straight, Karl!" he said to himself.

The King had humiliated him only at the behest of Aster, who had poured doubts into his mind.

He had not expected to see ancient travelers on Earth, yet he was not surprised to see Aster there. Around three millennia ago, before his home planet Hermes had learned to harvest gamma rays, there had been a power struggle. Back then, Captain Karl had been a simple Sergeant in the Hermtites military but prided himself on keeping informed about the upper hierarchy's dealings.

At that time, two of his fellow Hermetites had tried to rebel against their current captain in charge by gathering an army of rogue, Hermetites. They had almost been successful, but the military had stopped the targeted assassination before they could engage it. The two who had orchestrated the rebellion were exiled into space with nothing except the clothes on their back and sentenced to death if they ever dared to return.

Captain Karl had been appointed to keep track of the exiles, reporting their whereabouts to the Elders. He discovered the two had survived peacefully on Earth and even had a child. Eventually, the two died of what the earthlings called old age. Back then, the conditions of Earth had been worse since it was right after the great destruction, and toxic fumes permeated the air for centuries after that. Some Earthlings had perished, whereas others had adapted. Both Aster's parents had succumbed to the toxins.

They convinced the Earthlings to adopt him, so the child could be raised amongst the Earth's locals, learning their customs and beliefs.

Captain Karl had known where Aster was, but he did not think he would have established a prestigious position amongst Earth's royalty. He never followed the child's progress, assuming the Earthlings were generally unmalicious, but he was proven wrong when King Howard refused an alliance because of him.

The Captain strategized a new narrative for his alliance, "if I gave in, avoiding the controversy, and leaving the planet behind, a number of my stubborn followers would rebel." He convinced himself they would clamor against him, claiming they initially agreed to come with him and risked the dangers of traveling billions of their calculated light years only because he had tempted them with Earth's endless resources."

He knew it was a weak argument at best, but he needed a firm conviction to follow through. Besides, it was easier to blame others if his diabolical plans took a turn for the worst.

"How dare they?" he demanded out loud, his voice ringing in the metallic chamber around him. "How dare they trust the progeny of a treasonous, long-gone Hermetite couple, instead of allying with me?"

Somehow, voicing out his frustrations made him feel better. The Earthlings had destroyed the Earth once, and they would destroy it again. He did not believe they deserved the Earth because all they did was raze any progress. Captain Karl had planned to rule the Earth from the start, but the Elders had ruined that plan. He could have killed all Earthlings had it not been for the Elders, who insisted that a peaceful approach would be more viable long-term.

On planet Hermes they had a simple governing system. There were civilians and there were troops to control them.

At the annual Elders meeting of the (H.C.R.B.H), Hermatites Countrymen Representing the Betterment of Herme's,

Captain Karl proposed new ideas to expand their territory and occupy other worlds. Exercising better control of the civilians, making them a more potent military force, and since the panel of Elders had complete control, they would either veto or accept his ideas. Karl called it a (Keeping the Peace project)

When Captain Karl first mentioned the idea of occupying Earth, the Elder had been sorely against it. They did not believe it would lead to anything other than more destruction. Somehow, despite his silver tongue, Captain Karl had not been able to convince them. He did not have a good way of explaining to his peace-loving Elders that the Earthlings had destroyed many of the planet's resources. He would propose a plan to economize the Earthlings to colonize the country and save them from themselves.

He sighed. He was not a patient man. He had been taught the value of hard labor. His work ethic had given him the incentive to achieve many things. He had set his sights on Earth from the very start. Being a Captain, self-appointed as it was, wasn't enough. Once he took over Earth and made himself King, his demands would be simple knowing Earth was vulnerable, and would easily follow a strong leader.

To seal the deal, the Hermetites' weaponry, had the potential to permanently destroy the lands and completely wipe out all races on it, exactly like they had done with the red planet. The only catch was how to access the weapons. Unfortunately, the Elders controlled it all, and they only allocated its use to requesters that benefited a peaceful objective. Seems Karl needed an alternative backup plan. Luckily for him, multitasking was always his method of operation. He knew what he needed to do.

'One step at a time' He thought. Somehow he had to convince the Elders that his intentions were good. The Hermetite council did not approve of hostile takeovers. And finding enough trusted troopers might be difficult. *'I'll let my two minions figure that one out.'* Karl thought. They can schmooze as well as I can; after all, I taught

them everything they know. Besides, I have a bigger problem to solve.

The floor was solid, but his shoes barely made a sound. The entire ship was designed to absorb sound for silent maneuvering. It was also how they built their power units, soundless and sleek. The whole ship was powered by solar energy and gamma technology, something they had only recently developed. Their species had learned to harvest gamma radiations and use them to power their ships. It was a hundred times more efficient than the old nuclear energy.

Sitting at the circular table, at the Herme's council, Captain Karl informed his superiors of his intentions.

At the initial meeting, he showed them a map of the Earthlings' civilization.

"This, my comrades, is the local territory I intend to secure," he said.

"Secure?" one of his guards asked. "Did we not plan (over-the-table) cooperation? I believe we intended an alliance. We swore upon it, so why are you going against the plan?"

"They are not as we expected them to be. They've let their planet deteriorate and destroyed any valuable resources. Then, to make matters worse, they called war upon us, claimed they would refuse an alliance, and now, we have no choice but to secure the boundaries and govern properly," Captain Karl said.

That had been Karl's plan all along, but because of the

Elder's insistence on peace, he had conceded. Did they want him to first ally with the Earthlings and then establish a colony? Resulting in a peaceful takeover of Earth? He chuckled at the so-called passive proposal. "*Who has that kind of time?*" he thought. "It would surely lead to more problems.

"Force is against our ethics, Captain. Our morality does not allow us to execute force over any being, superior or inferior," the Guard continued, frustrated.

"I understand," Captain Karl said patiently. "Don't call it force, call it push back, but if we restrict our forces, the creatures who came before us will demand their injunction. They are not people like you and me. These are creatures that worship war. If they think the Earthlings refused our alliance, they will declare war, first against the Earthlings, and then start a rebellion against us."

Karl used the exaggerated version of a fabricated excuse for what he truly wanted. He knew that outright war was an easier option, and after the extreme humiliation he had faced, by the King Howard, he was eager to see the destruction of the entire race. It was hard for him to speak peacefully, with a straight face. His conscience did not bother him, but being forced to put on a peace-loving façade irked him immensely.

'How dare a weak…. useless species disrespect me?' he thought angrily, being cautious not to speak out loud. He needed to be in the Elder's good graces if he wanted their continued support.

"Yes!," an Elder agreed after a moment's thought.

"I Will say this. The Elders are the most brilliant minds of the millennia. We put nothing, in the way of science. If we oppose them, they may turn our own technology back on us. We would be helpless against it."

"I know," Captian Karl said, pretending to be worried. Each Hermetite servant had a small chip embedded in their head, and Captain Karl had the switch. He had only to press a button to activate and put them into a comatose state if any got out of hand. He also knew that the Elders had complete control over all his forces. Their command overruled his, and the military would instinctively obey the Elders over him. The Elders could strip him of his title if he stepped out of line.

Their species was primarily a peace-loving one, despite their militarized government systems. They had created a perfect establishment where no individual went without sustenance or shelter, so they were involved in peaceful self-actualization. Unfortunately, the bullheaded Captain Karl never followed the system. He had a system of his own.

"We must remove the threat before they threaten our tranquil existence. Captain Karl said, trying to convince his Elders that war was the answer.

The military forces, though brilliant, believed that advancement was the goal. They were alright with controlled confrontation, as long as it meant progress. These were the very forces Captain Karl had been appointed to control.

"You're right," another Guard said gravely. "War is our only option." They had not wanted to agree to war because they knew peace was always a better decision, but they had no choice. He refused to have his Captain be disgraced in that manner."

"Especially in the middle of a peaceful negotiation," Karl added.

Back on Earth, Karl stood up and made his way through the cold passages of the enormous ship. It was always kept at a regulated, constant temperature lower than Earth's. The Hematites were more adapted to the cold. Captain Karl found the heat extremely suffocating and attributed it to the planet's great destruction. Nuclear dust was still trapped in the atmosphere, making it several degrees warmer than it should have been.

There was no communal address system on the ship, except for the devices attached to each Hermetites' head.

When he switched it on, all or chosen Hermetite could hear his instructions. He reached out to the middle of his forehead, tapped it twice to activate the technology, and then focused on visualizing his password, which prompted him to speak. Once that was done, he gave his mental instructions to connect to the minion of his choice. *'A much better way to code military secrets.'* He thought. *'Information on a need-to-know basis, only to the ones needing to know.*

"Prepare our weaponry, load the ship, and complete all invasion procedures. We must infiltrate their base before we open an attack."

`Captain Karl caught one of the Elder's eyes and quickly switched to vocalizing, "If there is a way to get their resources peacefully, we must use that option. Remember, we must maintain peace at every possible level."

Kark knew how to poor on the sarcasm. His voice was firm, as he hid a slight smirk.The Elders had had their turn when they decided on peace, and it was time for him to start a war.

He knew the Earthlings fought over gold and riches and brought their destruction through their greed for wealth. Once he overtook Earth, absorbed their wealth, and became their new King, he would not only be filthy rich, he would be saving the planet from itself. However, if the Elders refused to help, he would have been forced to turn to the gruesome, ugly pirates. Those disgusting species that had landed on Earth before them might be his last resort.

Elders were derived from older Hermetite judges, arbitrators, and soldiers alike, who had served in both military and government positions for their entire careers. Now, after seeing the corruption of what hate and moral enemies can do to people, they have a deep passion for peace. They have the power to make and enforce the rules of the land, and only they have the authority to call for the punishment of death of the convicted whenever they felt it appropriate. With that kind of power, they were elected solely on their morals and rational decision-making. No Elder would ever give in to jealousy or greed. No bleeding hearts were allowed with the Elders. An Elder could only be removed if the protocol was breached. The code of conduct was strict. One did not defy an Elder, although Karl always seemed to find his way around them.

'Soon, I will no longer be just a Captain,' he thought, with a small smile. 'I will be King of the Earth. And all those who underestimated me then will bow before me. He strode out of the meeting room, leaving the Elders behind him.

"He is a volatile Captain," Elder Samuel commented. "Perhaps it was wrong for us to appoint him as one."

Ezra, another one of the Elders, spoke up.

"Trouble is brewing in the cosmos. The celestial bodies are misaligned, and I suspect that the streaks of light we now see across the night sky are the beginnings of a galaxy catastrophe soon."

CHAPTER 4

THE PIRATES

Tchaka paced across the ship's upper deck, his heavy iron boots scraping the floor, but he did not seem to notice the chilling sound it created. "Harder. Fight harder!" he commanded, watching his men below sparring with each other.

Piratoon had been overwrought with war for as long as Tchaka could remember. Greed and power had consumed the hierocracy. Without it, they were nothing but workers and enslaved people. The less fortunate ones lived underground and only came up to work for the elite. (The Grounders) as they were referred to, were not allowed to speak to the elite. Only to answer if spoken to. Many had died trying to gain a foothold above but were usually executed before they gained any momentum. Life on Piratoon was grand for some, hell for others. The name Pirate was given to individuals as a title of honor bestowed upon them in recognition of their merit. To be called a Pirate was to be honored. Not too many grounders aspired to be a Pirate. Even though the name was noble, the dangers were not.

Tchaka had barely been fifteen when he and his father were relocated to planet Earth after their world had been ravaged by constant war and famine waged through the land. He had seen combat, participated in it, and learned strategic fighting and military methods. By mimicking his superiors, he knew how to assemble intricate weaponry before he could speak. That was the custom of the pirate children and how they were raised.

He had been one of the youngest to settle on Earth after his father, Sinkara, took command of the Pirates and made himself a leader, and in turn, was treated as such by his subordinates. Initially, due to being on Earth and away from the malicious activity of Piratoon, they were compelled to live in peace. Still, the Pirates were a terrible, fighting species, and the consensus was not kept for long.

As the pirate population grew, requiring more resources for their fighting force, they started capturing vulnerable earthlings and using them at their discretion. They preferred slavery and manual labor, but a fast-moving target was considered an asset in a young Pirate's weapons training.

Tchaka thought the locals were beneath him, and he was not above capturing Earthling children for leverage. After he had regrouped his clan, he started doing the same procedure to train his army.

However, capturing live Earthlings became more complex once they started fighting back. Sinkara had raised his son with the same temperament. He'd take Tchaka on expeditions, as he called them, to the earthling villages, where he would command his allegiance to kill any encountered Earthlings along the way,

A pirate was not a species one wanted to go near. Eventually, the Earthling King had grown weary of the constant bloodshed in his land and waged war against the Pirates, using fire and brimstone to remove them.

They managed to overpower a significant Pirate village, driving them to the very edge of the shore where they had originally landed. The Pirates' one weakness was the fire which was also why most of them were massively averse to heat and preferred staying near bodies of water.

Tchaka's father had perished in that early war. The only thing Tchaka could use to identify his father's corpse was the ring he took that was still attached to his father's charred finger. Tchaka looked down at the sparring warriors, then looked away, lifting his hand to the light so it could glint off his metallic ring. He had sworn to take revenge. His father had been a terrible man who had advocated war, killed off many of his own, instigated a rebellion on Piratoon, ordered the death of hundreds of innocents, and committed treason and mutiny, all in his wake.

But that was an accepted ritual for a Pirate since they were, by nature, war-loving creatures. They believed in a 'kill or be killed' mentality and would do anything to win.

Pirates had no moral values since they believed everything was fair game and felt they deserved anything they could steal or confiscate from anyone, especially those more fortunate than themselves. Sinkara had been one of the clan leaders on his home planet, and his philosophy was, "We must take from the weak to prove our strength, for if the weak cannot protect what they have, then it is our responsibility to take it and raise our status by reminding them of our superior strength."

Piratoon had never had any functioning government system. The rich, the talented, and the most provocative would influence groups, create clans and fight for land resources. Sinkara quickly fell into that circle. He sincerely enjoyed his acquired sense of power.

The clans were often disorganized since their leaders never bothered to inform them of anything, but being uninformed was accepted by the clan members if only to be a part of the powerful elite.

A Pirate was assigned a clan during their youth, which required commitment and loyalty for the rest of their lives. The only way out of the family was death. The most prominent clan had belonged to Sinkara, which meant Tchaka had inherited extreme riches as a child. Since Pirates were primarily a very Spartan society, it also told that they were no strangers to pain. His father had taught him to wield weapons in both hands. When Sinkara noticed his son's left hand was weaker, he broke his right hand to strengthen his left one. As a result, Tchaka became ambidextrous, or as the Pirates called it, a Lefty Righty.

He was rumored to be a highly valued warrior that swung both ways, infuriating Tchaka.

Tchaka believed that his father's harsh training methodology had only made him more robust and equipped to handle opponents. That was how he was raised, and he knew it was the only way to survive in a cutthroat world amongst a species as bloodthirsty as the Pirates. He, too, believed in his father's ideology and was inclined toward war.

Although Sinkara and a few critical warriors in the clan had been killed, the younger, Tchaka, had survived. He had re-assembled the broken, wandering survivors and launched the exhausting search for a new strategic location this time, with better resistance to adversity.

They had started as a small party of fifteen, with only five women and three children. In time, their small party grew. For the first few years of their primitive lifestyle, they resided in caves, hiding and surviving on the flesh of stray animals.

One of the first things Tchaka did was invoke vigorous training to ensure his warriors were familiar with the Pirate's crucial military maneuvers. Eventually, the clan's young children grew older, and the population grew. Once Tchaka saw the abilities of his fighting clan, he realized they were ready to start plundering villages. That's when he began to plan his strategies, following the formula devised by his ancient ancestors.

He loved his father immensely, but he had to admit that his father had been slightly tactless. He resolved to have a more subtle approach, doing things more stealthily. He was more of a tactician, whereas his father had been a spontaneous dictator, so he knew he would succeed over his father.

"The clan needs to work together as one if we want to rise against the King," Tchaka said, continuing his tirade. "Don't forget the wars your forefathers have fought."

Pirates were generally unsympathetic to death and didn't acknowledge or mourn the losses resulting from the residuals of war. However, blood family at the higher levels was the only exception. Winning was the main objective of a committed pirate.

"We lost a battle, but the war is yet to be won. We must fight for revenge," Tchaka continued.

The allegiance nodded to his words, echoing the word 'REVENGE!' after he finished speaking. He surveyed them and smiled. His forces consisted of males and females starting from ages as young as twelve to a hundred and forty-eight. Since the Pirates had acclimatized themselves to war, they had extremely long lifespans, which was another advantage. His father had been two-hundred and eighty-one when he had been killed. Tchaka was still considerably young, having been alive for only a century, but he was convinced that he was wiser than most of the oldest members of the clan.

Most of his leadership qualities had been inherited from his father. He had been the one to reorganize the clan and lift them up to war-like readiness. It was something he was immensely proud of.

He had inspired the development of new weaponry, some of which was still raw, unable to function as well as the ones he had seen in his childhood, but it was still better than anything the Earthlings possessed. One of the weapons was a long, cylindrical tube filled with a compact projecting cartridge, when ignited, shot a laser strong enough to cut completely through a body's torso.

Another weapon was a sphere buried into the ground and then activated by an unsuspecting traveler. When stepped on, it would explode, in a fiery blaze loaded with a chemical compound, instantly killing its victim. Then all that was needed after that was to scavenge the bodies for valuables if there were any left.

The metal alloy was their most used resource since it was used in making tools and weapons. Tchaka hoped that none of the Earthlings ever discovered the metallurgical knowledge of their own making. Since the Earthlings vastly outnumbered the Piratoons, if they ever managed to replicate the Piratoon weapon technology, Pirates would no longer have the advantage, and the Battle of the Dorsal Sea, where his father was defeated, desperately needed the edge for a victorious retaliation.

"Tchaka!" one of the men came running up, his breath heavy.

He had been sent to spy on the Earthling king. It was difficult for Pirates to be spies because they looked vastly different from humans. They had narrower chests since they required lesser oxygen and sharper teeth for tearing into flesh. They were short men, stubby, and a prominent hip bone that jutted out at an awkward angle, Noticeable to those who cared to observe.

However, most were often unclean, streaked with pus-filled wounds and scabs from wars and fights. Many of them had missing limbs, some had missing noses or ears, and one of them, a skirmish older Pirate, had lost both ears!

Their skins were slightly blue, and their veins were more

prominent since their blood was a silvery blue, whereas Garnish had bounced between Pirate and Earthling's children, playing and getting accepted through his childhood.

The Pirates mostly communicated through clicks and various grunting sounds that defined their language. They are sophisticated enough within their own culture but come across as primitive to anyone else. They also used crude hand gestures to talk to each other, considered pirate slang, since most of the motions were usually cursing words or plans to create chaos.

Garnish, however, had played among the earthling children, so he had picked up their language and could communicate with them. Funnily enough, he had also taught the Earthling children rude gestures that were later carried down from generation to generation. Apart from being a spy, Garnish was also an invaluable translator for Tchaka and his troops.

"Garnish?" Tchaka asked, not expecting to see the young man.

Being a hybrid, blending in with the locals was easy. He despised the Earthling's politics since the village had brutally executed his Earthling mother once they had discovered she had consummated with a Pirate and bore a son. Ignoring the fact that it had been a rape, the town convicted her anyway.

Garnish somehow managed to kill his father in a rage that escalated into a physical confrontation over the mourning of his human mother, whom he had never met.

Being unsympathetic to death, his father minimized his loss.

Garnish was raised by Tchaka. He had been one of the few who survived the war and one of Tchaka's earliest recruits.

"Tell me, Garnish, what news do you bring?" Tchaka asked.

"The Earthling King dishonored the Hermetite Captain, Sir, and had him escorted from his court. The captain has declared war on the King. I believe our time has come," Garnish said once he had regained his breath.

Tchaka laughed, a choking sound similar to a fish flopping against a wooden floor.

"Our time has come, indeed. We must ready our forces. Let us see how the fearsome Earthlings can fend off two species simultaneously," he said, looking appraisingly at his troops.

The Hermetites had recently traveled to the planet, so they were a mystery, although the turn of events seemed interesting to Tchaka. Pirates were a very particular breed, Tchaka would never entertain the idea of an alliance with a species like the Hermetites. They were much too inferior to him, but he was not above taking advantage of the any situation. If the Hematites attacked the King, they would, ensure his victory over the weakened Earthlings.

"I will finally be able to take revenge." He twisted the ring on his finger, the only remaining memoir of his father, and with a whisper, he closed his eyes. "I shall avenge you, father. I shall slaughter the Earthling King myself."

CHAPTER 5

CLAIM TO POWER

At the last meeting with Herme's highest pinnacle of Elders, Karl rehearsed his proposal. This would be the final decision. No more preliminaries, no more changes, and most importantly, no more rehearsed speeches. After this, if he couldn't convince the upper echelon, he would be on his own. He stood in the Elder's council hall, looking down at the principal city of his home planet, Hermes, and surveying it with pride. He was the one who had helped maintain order there for so long. Throughout his time, Captain Karl had served brilliantly, won numerous medals, and been victorious at every new control strategy. Despite the glory, he wanted more. Karl was no longer content with being the captain; his dream was to rule a planet like the Elders led Hermes. Except, he wanted to be the sole ruler.

However, Karl knew that he could never gain control of Hermes as long as the Elders lived. So, as a result, he had set his eyes on Earth and the countless rich bounties it offered. It was not as rich as his advanced home planet, but it had its charm.

Hermes was littered with tall buildings that blocked out the light of the two suns, but that barely mattered because it was lit up by bright lights that were rarely turned off. The buildings had a metallic exterior and were welded together with solidified mercury, having an architectural allure that could be marveled by any Hematite gazing up from ground level. Its streets were paved with manganese iron which provided maglev-repelling currents that aided in helping their vehicles travel extremely fast in their small pods.

From where Captain Karl was standing, the pods looked distant and small, like spherical droplets of water streaking across the polished tracks. He sighed contentment before turning away, anxiously wondering when the Elders would arrive. He had come early, mainly because he wanted time to psych up beforehand to counter any negative negotiations. Confident and eager, Karl was known for dominating a debate. The Elders had already begrudgingly agreed, somewhat to Karls war. Still, he feared they would turn back on their decision at the last moment, and he could not afford that, especially not when he had come so far.

He had been focusing on Earth's governing authorities, assuring his diabolical plans were feasible and, most of all, failsafe. He knew the Earthlings would not stand a chance against Hermes' high technology, which the Elders could provide him once they allowed him access to its armament.

Captain Karl specifically wanted Earth because of how different it was from Hermes. It was undeveloped, with raw beauty, animals, plants, birds, and fishes. Hermes barely had any vegetation, and their diet mainly consisted of nutrients they had learned to harvest through neutron collider technology. Other animals, unable to adapt to the planet's cold, metallic structure, eventually died out and became extinct.

The double doors behind Captain Karl opened, and he turned around, smiling as the elders filed in. He glanced at Samuel, the kindest Elder, who beckoned for him to start.

"Gracious Elders," Karl began, "I heartily thank you for allowing me here. I have come to discuss the terms of my invasion of Earth. I have come to understand that your troops will aid me."

The Elders nodded, and Elder Ezra said, "You understand correctly, captain. We will allow you to use 120 Laser Weapons, 150 Electric Fields, and 200 men."

Captain Karl smiled victoriously, realizing that it would be enough. The laser weapons were triangular objects that boasted a hundred-percent kill shot guarantee at any moving target within a 100-unit circumference. The only drawback was that the targets had to be moving for the lasers to detect them. However, the captain was confident that the unintelligent Earthlings could not deduce this.

Electric Fields were baton-like objects that electrocuted someone when they touched their bare skin. Laser Weapons were used for long-range targets, and he was sure the human swords, bows, and arrows were no match for the Electric Fields.

"That is all I will need," the captain told them as he bowed his head in gratitude.

The Elders sat on stools surrounding a hovering metal

slab that served as a table. Captain Karl, however, was standing to show them respect. He tried to leave the room through the side door, being too hasty to wait for the leaders to dismiss him when Vienna, the most senior Elder, called out, "We are not done!"

Captain Karl turned around. He hated Vienna primarily because she had the most power out of all of them and knew it. She had been distrustful of him since the beginning, claiming that power often got to his head and that having him as a captain was dangerous. Yet, she had begrudgingly let him keep his title.

"I apologize, Elder Vienna," he said, trying to mask his anger but failing miserably.

"You take one step out of line Captain Marx Karl and I will ensure you are stripped of your title and reduced to a mere civilian. You are not to manipulate your troops in any way. And you are to report to us directly through the external communication links we sent you. I am told you set them up around Earth? See to it that they are all operational. It would be best if you first attempted a peaceful confrontation. Your death count must be minimal during this time. However, if war breaks out, you can defend as required. But, if I find any evidence of foul play on your part, you will be prosecuted to the fullest. During your endeavor, you are not to offensively attack, only counter if you get attacked. Understood?"

Vienna didn't trust Captain Karl, but she had to comply with the rest of the panel of Elders, most of whom held Captain Karl in high esteem because he had captured and eliminated the rebel forces of Aster's parents years ago. She knew Karl was not to be trusted but she had no words on which to base her feelings. "Just a gut feeling" she would say.

Herme's resources were quickly running out, and Earth was the only planet close enough with any usable resources suitable. They used to consume animal meat, but the development of their elegant cities was replacing the animal habitats. Earth was accessible enough to hunt the fields and still be able to transport the yield back to Hermes. Lithium-ion was another mineral they needed for their metro transportation. The Elders wanted to partner with Earth, not overtake it.

Captain Karl suppressed his grimace and nodded his head once. "Understood," he repeated.

"This court meeting is dismissed," the Elders murmured.

Captain Karl finally left, exiting the metallic buildings and stepping onto the magnetic streets. His two bodyguards stepped beside him as soon as he stepped out, having waited outside till he finished his meeting with the Elders.

Looking at them, Captain Karl found himself smiling. They were two of his very own men, brainwashed to the point of submission, and he knew they were one of the very few people who would dare to go against the elders. Most civilians and military personnel blindly followed the elders. Ironically preaching for Peace, yet training for war. On the other hand, Captain Karl thought that war was necessary to attain true peace because his version of 'peace' meant 'absolute control.'

"Is the Ship prepared for take-off? he asked his bodyguards.

"Yes, Captain," one of them echoed obediently, not a hint of emotion in his voice.

"Excellent!" Captain Karl murmured. "Load it with exactly 120 Laser Weapons and 150 Electric Fields. Then, pick 200 of their best soldiers to take back to Earth."

"Yes, Captain," the other bodyguard said and slinked away into the shadows, his metallic outfit blending in with the sheen of the buildings.

"They knew that Vienna would have never given Karl 200 of her best soldiers, but agreed to play along.

Once everything was prepared, Captain Karl boarded, announcing to his army of 200 to prepare for take-off and hold on to the stabilizing bars that ran along the entire corridor. In a few moments, the ship blasted off toward the galaxy, making its way toward the one planet he had decided to conquer.

Captain Karl grinned in absolute delight when he got the first glimpse of Earth.

At closer range, he could see the coastline of the great ocean and pre-tuned the ship's navigational coordinates.

He would need to hide the ship this time.n He needed to be even more stealthy now since his plan was going into action. Luckily, he had visited the sea once before and knew that most underwater caves had huge openings to enter a vessel his size while being relatively safe from whales and giant aquatic beasts.

The ship finally settled, into an enormous underwater cavernous cave. How convenient, he thought, it was a good plan. Once settled in out of sight, Captain Karl started hatching his first plans against the Earthlings. The Hematites had similar features to humans, and he knew the best plan of action, would be to infiltrate.

Captain Karl debated going in, destroying the front lines of Howard's army, and storming into the castle. The idea of razing the King's palace right before him while he sat bound to his throne was satisfying. The humiliation of being kicked out of the castle was fresh in Captain Karl's head, and he fanaticized about torturing the Earthling King in the same manner. However, he also knew that he could not step out of line. The Elders had eyes everywhere since they had their spies. If he acted impulsively or attacked the Earthlings, they would stop the support coming his way. Or worse, come after him.

He made his way to his chambers. Even though the rest of the ship was a bright, white metallic color, his space was a dimly lit metal alloy since he preferred the shadowed darkness. His bodyguards were already waiting for him when he made his way inside.

"Tatun. Rye," Captain Karl greeted, simply by uttering their names.

The two immediately stood. Tatun and Rye were brothers who had been in the military since they were pre-teens and had worked for him for over forty years. They were his late sister's sons, and when they had become orphaned, Captain Karl had no other option but to take them in. However, he was utterly inept at raising younglings and enlisted them into the military.

The captain's comrades assumed he had adopted the twin boys out of the goodness of his heart, but the truth was, he always saw them as someone he could groom to be his spies and minions. He was proud of how he had brainwashed them into the perfect warriors, so much so that they were the only ones who would rise against the elders without fear. They would be willing to take the blame for his actions if he ever got in trouble. It was a very convenient relationship with no emotional ties. And yet, he still felt affection for his two little Fall Guys.

"Do you have a report for me?"

"Yes, Captain," Rye said in his usual monotone drawl. "The ship had been secured within the conduit of an underwater cavern. The cave has had a trapped air bubble inside and relatively low cyclone activity for the past two hundred years, so there is a triple aught 2% chance of one forming now. Moreover, the ship's technology has been retested, so the metal will not be harmed even if the water line or temperature fluctuates. As long as we are inside it, we'll be out of sight and safe."

"Excellent," Captain Karl said. He walked across the floor and settled himself onto an impromptu throne. He figured the wait to get the Earthling King's throne was too long, and he was impatient. "And what of our infiltration?"

Tatun hesitated before answering him. "The infiltration

is underway. Our troops have found it difficult to blend in with the human masses. Certain differences are too huge to be ignored."

"What differences?" Captain Karl snapped.

Tatun winced at the outburst.

"Our voices are slightly deeper than most human voices. Apart from that, our completions are pale. Humans have more sun exposure. The lack of sun exposure on Hermes due to the high buildings blocking out light has kept us light-skinned. Lastly," Tatun stopped speaking, touched the tips of his pointed ears, and winced. "They're pointed."

Captain Karl clenched his jaw. "Have none of you got any semblance of intelligence? Drat you! A mere Earthling could devise the solution to these. First, Speak softer not to bring attention. Have the imposters go through UV lasers to tint the skin and the ears … cut them off for all I care."

"Captain, if I may," Rey politely suggested, "We use concealing liquid to hide our pointed ears." Concealing liquid was a camouflage material that the Hermetites had stumbled upon during their expeditions to one of the other planets. However, it was in a minimal amount. It had the property to deflect light so that the object behind it would be rendered completely invisible.

"Excellent," Captain Karl said. He pressed a button and brought up a hologram of the map of the Earthling territory. He located old man Aster's little cottage and zoomed into it.

"If we are doing this. We must bide our time and do it right, especially since the Elders insist that we do it the long way. The man living in this cottage is a Hermatite called

Aster. However, he knows nothing about our technology or our concealing methods. One of our strongest men should be placed here and gain Aster's trust and loyalty. We need another two men for the King's inner advisory council, and ten must join the Earthling's hunting forces."

Rye and Tatun stared at Captain Karl in awe. Anybody else would be disgusted by his thirst for vengeance, especially since most Hermatites were vast supporters of peace.

Conveniently, his bodyguards had been brainwashed to practically worship every decision he made, a practical skill Karl had learned to administer within his debates.

A few hours later, the preparation had been completed, and the Hematites were sent to their positions. It was decided that the King's two incognito advisors would be Tatun and Rye, while Captain Karl handled Aster himself. They could have easily stripped Earth of its resources if he had used his convincing skills on King Howard. Everything would have been easy for him if it had not been for Aster. Captain Karl also decided that he would need to assimilate into Earth's security regiments and randomly placed his 200 men within the confines of the fighting forces.

Becoming a King's advisor was easy. The Earthling hiring and qualification system were reasonably straightforward. They would be accepted if they could pass physical and mental tests. These tests were extremely easy for the two Hermetites; they were quickly selected.

Gaining Aster's trust was different. Despite the skin and facial-altering technology Captain Karl used, he knew that

Aster was a wise man and needed to be careful. He had the beginnings of a plan in mind, but he had yet to carry it out. Infiltrating the area had been relatively easy, but they had yet to establish a strategy to eradicate the Kingdom. And that could happen once Captain Karl managed to get Aster's trust.

"I may have to use brute force," he thought.

"No," he said, deciding. "I will have to do something else. Aster is too wise to trust a Hermetite or even an Earthling. Diplomatic diplomacy, along with a slight bit of evil interjection, might be required since it had always been his failsafe method of operation. He could easily let his bodyguards infiltrate the King's Advisory cabinet, but he also needed a foolproof backup plan to ensure everything went his way.

CHAPTER 6

THE BOY IS LOST

The palace was decked out in the finest decorations. Garlands hung across the pillars, and creeping lianas traversed the windows in full bloom. Wreaths of birch flowers and scented pink peonies hung from the ceiling, providing a splash of bright color to liven up the mood.

Walls contrasted by the clean floors, cleaned until they sparkled bright enough for the Earthlings almost to see their reflection. That was bridged by walls painted in a fresco style of luxurious Chapple's. When anyone stepped inside, they found themselves in a rough entryway where they had to prepare their feet coverings before entering to prevent anyone from slipping on the polished floor.

The entire community was preparing for the spring festival, and everyone was cheerful because all civilians were invited to the grand dance ceremony at the King's palace. Mothers dyed their white clothes with primitive indigo dyes while young girls found rogue and berries to color their lips. Young men practiced their dance steps, and fathers skittered about, finding gifts to thank the King for helping them support their families.

The community had a spring festival every five seasons, and it was always a grand occasion. All commoners were allowed, and the King gave a speech, thanking them for the devotion, loyalty, subservience, and hard work they had put in to grow their harvest and help prosper the township. The ones who had already attended the festival were eager to revisit it and occupied themselves with telling the younger ones stories about how beautiful it would be, increasing their expectations. The youngsters ran about the place, excited by the liveliness.

King Howard, too, anxiously memorized his speech in his stately chamber, realizing that many people would be listening to him. The festival was growing closer. At mid-afternoon, one of King Howard's men rang the massive bell in the village square seven times, signifying that the festival had begun.

The castle doors were thrown open, and the locals walked inside, marveling at the entertainment stalls set up for their benefit. After preparations, the old ruined palace was a piece of architectural genius, built with a vast courtyard, large enough to host a small army, should it be needed.

King Howard watched as his people milled about in throngs while he stood on the balcony with his young nephew.

"Uncle Howie, when will you give the speech?" his little nephew, Henry, asked.

"Soon, child, soon. Now hush and look at the domain you will one day rule over," King Howard said.

The King had no kids of his own. Already in the late stages of his life, he considered it too consuming a task to raise a child fit for the Kingdom. He was already training his nephew to be the next King, even though the child was only seven and knew little about anything.

After years of service as a village leader, Howard assumed the King's position but hoped to change that rule. It was one of the things he would declare in the ceremony. He wanted to make it so that the throne of the King would be passed down to the eldest heir of the passing King, and his heir was his little nephew, Henry.

While everyone was celebrating, Captain Karl's collusive forces were hard at work. His two bodyguards had already infiltrated the King's graces; they had known of his plan to pass on his only heir.

"Captain," Tatun whispered to his communicator. "The little boy will be taken from his chambers to the Main Hall while King Howard makes announcements. We need to work fast, distract the guards, and intercept the men leading Henry to the hall,"

He was standing in the Main Hall beside the King, preparing to speak.

Meanwhile, Henry had been sent to his chambers to be prepared but would be led forth any moment. Unfortunately, the King had hired guards stationed all around the palace.

"Noted. Troops, please take out the guards," Captain Karl said.

He had dressed as a commoner and blended in as a part of the crowd. Much to his displeasure, he had had to cut his hair and disguise his pointed ears. He loathed looking like one of them. His eyes were quick, noticing how every guard rapidly fell and was soon replaced by one of the disguised troops he had placed within the local crowd.

"Ladies and Gentlemen, welcome to the festival. It is my honor the …" King Howard said, but Captain Karl was not paying attention.

"Rye, status?" he demanded, speaking into the communication device on his wrist.

"We are on the way, Capitan Karl," Rye said. "I am with the guards escorting the little boy to the Main Hall. I will need assistance since they think I am a Royal Advisor and will be alerted if I appear instrumental in kidnaping the boy."

"I'll send assistance," Capitan Karl said. He communicated with his troops to ensure the guards with the boy were rendered unconscious. They also knocked out Rye since his position in the palace was valid, and it would have been slightly suspicious if he was the only one left standing. They could not afford to leave any traces behind.

Initially, little Henry did not realize what was happening, but then he started screaming, using all the strength his seven-year-old body offered.

Alas, he was no match for the adult Hermes who stuffed a gag inside his mouth, blindfolded him, and placed him in a huge trunk, which they carried to Captain Karl. When the captain saw the box being taken toward him, he smiled, knowing that half the plan was already underway.

He had anticipated the suspiciousness of a large trunk being carried away. Still, his fears were in vain since most locals were already taking huge packages out, filled with gifts they had won at the numerous game and food stalls inside the palace. He was not the only one with a trunk since many of the locals had them, too.

Sure enough, nobody stopped him as he carried the trunk out of the palace and left. Karl's men had already replaced the guards around the court and at the door.

"Ladies and gents," The King preceded. "I would like to present my nephew, your future King, Prince Henry!" as Howard unfolded his arm toward the corridor. That was the cue for Henry to be escorted into the Main Hall, but nobody appeared.

Unbeknownst to anyone else, Henry was struggling inside a trunk, already one-fourth of the way across the moors, carried by Captain Karl's troops. Captain Karl wasn't with them, but he knew what was happening at the palace because Tatun kept him informed about everything.

"Prince Henry?" the King called, but once again, nobody exited the antechamber connected to the main chamber, and he got worried. He beckoned to Aster, who was standing close behind him.

"Find out where the delay lies," he instructed Aster, who nodded and entered the palace hall.

When Aster saw the carnage around him; the guards on the floor with Advisor Rye passed out beside them, he shouted.

"Guards! What happened here? Where is Henry?" He yelled to the approaching men. He grabbed one of the injured, sitting him upright, and asked.

"Do you know who did this?

"I saw nothing, sir. It happened so fast.

Aster hurried back at a full run.

"The boy is lost," he whispered into the King's ear.

"What?" King Howard demanded, lowering his voice so as not to be heard.

"The boy has been taken. Nobody knows what happened. The guards and one of your advisors were all unconscious when I got there. It might have been an internal force, but I suspect it is the Hermetites," Aster said quickly, trying to explain everything in one quick breath, aware of the audience waiting for the King to continue his speech.

"My Dear God," the King said, his skin pale with fright. "A ransom, you suspect?" Howard's shaky voice was barely auditable. "I'll pay any demands, he said.

"King Howard, please. There is power in numbers. We can do it together," Aster suggested.

Howard nodded. "First things first," he said. "Inform your constituents."

Howard took a deep breath and slowly addressed the crowd.

"People, my little nephew, Prince Henry, has been abducted!" the King said, speaking over the whispers that had broken out. Again, he announced, hoping to get anything helpful "He is missing! He must be found. Every one of you must search the territory. There will be a handsome reward for his return." The King announced, trying not to stutter in his speech. Howard was terrified. Whoever had taken his nephew knew the ins and outs of the palace, and he hoped he would not have to face an internal betrayal.

Outside the palace, the bell started to toll. It rang once, twice, and then too many times to count. It was the kind of ringing that signified danger or problems. No one in the palace heard the bell ring. Perhaps because of the horrifying innocence that had just presented itself had shut down their conscience. At that point, nothing was obvious.

Captain Karl was nearing his ship. He commanded his transporter to take the trunk down to the submerged ship. By then the little guy had passed out from fear.

Captain Karl made sure to stay out of his sight. He did not want the child to recognize his features and later be able to identify him in any way. Little Henry was thrown into the cramped metallic room where Hermetites usually kept prisoners.

Rye had awakened and taken over the responsibility of consoling King Howard while Tatun and Aster stood back and watched.

"Don't worry. I believe one of the locals must have taken

him," Rye said as he lied through his teeth. "We will find the little Prince."

"The locals?" Aster snapped. "Pah! Do you think this kidnapping was the work of the Earthlings? No! This kidnapping has the Hermetites' smell all over it. I am certain they have a hand in it."

"I don't think they do-" Rye started to say but was interrupted by someone bursting through the door.

A village leader had rushed inside, panting, half bent over, and exclaimed, "The guards! All the guards at the gates and the ones surrounding the palace are down!"

King Howard stood up from his throne, terror seeping into his already weakened body.

"Down?" he demanded. "Any dead?"

He was concerned for his people and their families. For so long, he had ruled peacefully and seen his people progress. He resolved he would die trying to protect his them.

"No. No one is dead. Whoever did this was, making sure to only partially incapacitate!" the village leader stated.

Rye snorted but then quickly disguised it as a cough. Luckily for him, everyone else was too frazzled to notice.

'Of course, nobody was dead. If anyone were killed, the Elders would call Captain Karl back almost immediately,' Rye thought.

"Did anyone see anything?" Rye asked, pretending to be confused.

"I believe they were guard imposters. It was a planned covert attack.

"No witnesses," the village leader said, shaking his head regretfully.

Over the next few days, the locals thoroughly searched the King's territory, no stone was left unturned. They employed trained dogs to sniff out the King's nephew but to no avail.

All the tracking dogs would go to the sea and lose track from there. Nobody guessed that the kidnappers might have gone underwater since Earthlings did not possess such technology. It was unfathomable for them to think it was possible for anything to survive underwater. However, they didn't know how wrong they were.

Captain Karl bid his time, waiting until the King was most desperate. Just the thought of the putrid little King suffering made his day, and adding to the euphoria knowing he was causing it, felt even better.

"I'll let him worry about that for a while." He thought. He'd make his move once he was sure fear and desperation had set in.

CHAPTER 7

UNBOWED

Darius and Settii eavesdropping from a distance as the hunting group sat together and talked. At fifteen, they were too young to hunt with the others, but they still had the thirst to be part of something greater. They, too, wanted to hunt food for their village and bring it glory. They envied Bakaii, who sat around the fire and proudly talked with the others, having already been initiated into the group three years ago.

"I bet the aliens took little Prince Henry," Bakasii snarled, and the hunting team nodded. This was the exact kind of gossip they liked hanging around to hear.

"Yeah, Brother. But let's not make assumptions," one of the older men said with a sigh.

Bakaii took a huge bite of his chicken and muttered, "They have probably been waitin' to stir up some horse dung ever since King Edward kicked them out. I know it."

"We don't even know who they are!" one of the men said.

"Don't you know?" Bakaii asked between chews. He

lowered his voice. "They come from the sea, don't they? They have the boats that sink deep in water, don't they?"

"Boats that can go beneath the water?" one of the adults asked and then snorted. "That's crazy! Boats can only go under the water if they are broken. Are you suggestin' they are the ghosts of men drowned at sea?"

There was a round of laughter, and Bakaii blushed with embarrassment.

"They come from the sea, I tell ya!" he insisted.

"So, like sea people?" one of the younger men on the hunting party asked.

Bakaii nodded.

"Exactly! Don't they come from the sea? I say they are sea people!" he said confidently.

"Sea People it is, then," one of the adults said.

A bug crept up on Settii's leg, and he swatted it away, but the movement alerted the hunting team.

"Who's there?" one of the men asked.

"Run," Darius mouthed, although they weren't breaking the rules this time. Still, the two turned and ran out of habit.

After stopping to catch their breath, Settii softly said, "Why are we running?"

However, that was not the last they would hear of the so-called Sea People.

Captain Karl was incensed.

"What do you mean we are running out of sustenance?" he demanded.

"The sea seems to be dying because of our ship. Fish, aquatic and marine life has decreased drastically, Captain. We are not sure how long it will be before we need to turn to eat vegetable produce," one of his men informed him.

He pinched the bridge of his nose and seated himself back in his comfortable chair, wishing Tatun and Rye could handle these minuscule engineering problems. However, they were both still pretending to be advisors for the King and were needed in the Earthling-occupied areas.

"I have no use for marine life. If it dies, so be it. If the salt content kills them, so be it. We can steal the land-grown produce that the Earthlings have after plundering their villages," he said.

"But- That would ... would mean we are harming the environment. This is what the Elders feared. We were supposed to do this without hurting the Earth in any way. The resources here are needed for the survival of our entire race. Will you jeopardize it like this then?" his soldier argued.

"That was then, this is now. The Elders don't need to know about this," he snapped. Seeing the startled look on the soldier's face, he changed his tone.

"We are doing what is necessary. Remember, I am doing this for the greater glory of Hermes so that we can have a resource-filled planet and co-exist with the Earthlings like the Elders wanted. You need to trust me and my decisions. I know what is at stake, too. Besides, we are only borrowing the crops, not depleting the land," he lied.

'Plundering' is not a peaceful coinage," Captain Karl mused.

He realized he needed to be more careful with his words. He had almost given away his real intentions - to wipe out the locals and dominate the planet.

"Yes, Captain," his soldier sighed and excused himself.

"This won't do," Captain Karl said as soon as he was alone. "These do-gooders have no personal ambition. It's terrible."

There was another knock at the door, and Captain Karl saw red. He was sick and tired of attending to people and wanted to murder whoever was at the door, especially if they were going to bring him minor, petty concerns.

"What is it?" he barked, and one of his soldiers stuck his head inside the door.

"Captain, we have heard of extra-terrestrials, apart from us, who have dominated the Earth and have been hiding out for a while," the man informed him.

"A while? Be specific, soldier. How long?" he demanded.

"For around five hundred years," the soldier said, and Captain Karl stiffened.

"Five hundred years, and they haven't been discovered?" he asked.

"Not so, Captain. The Earthling drove them to this very ocean, battled it out, and burned their ships. Some of them survived and have been secretly regrouping for around a century and a half," the soldier said.

"Leave me!" Captain Karl said, and the soldier hurried away, closing the door behind him.

He communicated to his spies via his chip technology and found out that the other extra-terrestrials were from a planet known as Piratoon, and their leader was a Pirate who went by the name Tchaka.

"I suppose we will need to pay these so-called terrestrials a little bit of a visit," he murmured.

He did not need the Pirates' assistance but knew they would be invaluable allies. Captain Karl was knowledgeable, and he almost always had at least multiple backup plans for every circumstance. He decided he needed to know more about the Pirates and meet this Tchaka for several reasons.

First, he needed to know more about the Pirates and their technology and build a connection between them to exchange technology and trade. That would also cover the lack of sustenance since he could make a deal with the Pirates and get them to farm for him in exchange for resources.

He could never risk the Pirates ever going against the Hermetites. Since Piratoon technology was quite advanced, though not as advanced as Hermetian technology, there was a slight chance there would be severe consequences if the Pirates attacked them. He needed to ensure that the Pirates were on their side and a mutual enemy of the Earthlings.

Lastly, if the Elders ever learned about the trickery Captain Karl had planned, and if they took away his forces and weaponry, he could depend on the Pirates' alliance. If the Pirates proved useless, there would still be no harm in allying with them and destroying them later when he was done using their forces.

It was with all this planning that he finally stood up and gathered five of his soldiers, jetting them from the ship on a dual submersible, knowing, but not caring, that to any Earthling, it would appear to be a ghost ship emerging from the water, he quickly made his way through the marshes and to Tchaka's territory.

He was met, first, by the official Pirate translator, Garnish, who seemed to be a half-earthling.

'A product of rape, indubitably,' Captain Karl assumed, noticing his characteristics.

The Pirates lived in low ling area's near damp caves of low mountains, where they were out of the way of any aliens, and Captain Karl cleverly noted there must have been a reason for that. He knew that they were, at one time, an advanced species that had mastered the ability of space travel; it was apparent they had regressed to a lower level of lifestyle.

He was sorely disappointed, however, when he saw Tchaka, who communicated in nothing except grunts and gestures. He had expected the Pirate leader to be a bit more sophisticated.

"I come in peace," Captain Karl stated, and Garnish translated it for Tchaka, who grunted back.

"Leader says he doesn't care. What do you guys want?" Garnish translated.

"We know you dislike King Howard. We, too, dislike him and want to end his rule. I want to join forces with you to strike together. Together, we will be unstoppable. We have the technology required for it, and so do you. The union would be invaluable to both parties," Captain Karl said confidently.

His convincing abilities allowed him the luxury of gathering alliances, Karl thought to himself as he waited for the translator's reply.

Tchaka made two short grunts in response, his face impassive and bored, seemingly unmoved by Captain Karl's offerings.

"No interest," Garnish translated, looking as bored as his leader.

"But then, with our merger … together, we can rule Earth!" Captain Karl insisted. "Together, we can destroy all of their forces."

Unbeknownst to Karl, Tchaka was not as interested in ruling the Earth as Karl was.

"Yeah. We gonna do that on our own, newbie," Garnish translated after waiting for Tchaka's responding grunts.

"Newbie?" Captain Karl asked, not knowing what the word meant, but a grimace crept up his lips. It had a weird sound. "Anyway, think of it. We have similar causes and grudges. We can take over!"

"No," Garnish translated. "Be gone, newbie. We don't need you."

Captain Karl raised his eyebrows. He was not used to informal talk, much less speech with words like 'be gone' and 'newbie,' phrases he had never heard before. His slick tongue usually affected others, but the Pirates were too irrational to communicate with.

Tchaka's war was personal. He was drowning in his

need for revenge. He was not interested in making alliances or ruling the Earth. He just wanted blood, and he was going to do it himself. He did not want the help of some fancy, Hermetite who would most likely be trying to command him.

He stood up.

"Get the beggar outta here!" he said.

The Captain did not know those words. They had been interpreted through what Karl assumed to be a loose translation, but he understood the context. They were used to getting rid of someone, so they were fulfilling their purpose.

They did not sound rude enough, though, so to add insult, Tchaka made a crude hand gesture in Captain Karl's direction. It was a gesture that Karl knew was not intended to be good. It was, once again, just like his offer to the King, yet another rejection that angered him beyond belief.

"They will be killed!" he shouted as soon as he was out of the territory and making his way to The home ship. "How dare they? This was worse than the Earthlings! I want their blood. I want every single one of them dead.

He entered the ship and walked to his chambers, angrily throwing his belongings around. He knew his messes would be cleaned up by his little minions later. He just needed to vent his fury.

"I will kill every single one of them for the disrespect. How dare they? All they do is kill, maim, and destroy. Earthling villages and settlements were all destroyed, and Earthlings were raped. They have burrowed holes into the

Earth like pests, tried to dig up resources, and consumed them for nothing but war when the Earthyling might have used them to construct buildings. They have no shred of dignity or respect!" he yelled, and his voice echoed on the metallic surfaces of the wall and floor, magnifying his anger.

He failed to realize or accept that he, too, was trying to do the same. He wanted to kill all Earthlings and destroy their settlements.

He called a meeting, assembling everyone in the main hall. Avoiding the chips in their heads, he wanted to ensure they saw and heard his sincerity in his voice when he laid out his frustrations. He knew the Hermetites were not war-inclined, and it would not be easy.

"My dear comrades!" he said, careful not to use the word 'soldiers' since some of them disliked its negative connotations, despite Hermes being a majority military rule. "We will need to establish war upon the Pirates.

They demonstrate blood-thirsty characteristics. They plan to take over the Earth and destroy the villages, while we want nothing but peace. We have advocated for peace from the beginning, haven't we?"

The lies rolled off his tongue so easily that it was disgusting.

His soldiers nodded, agreeing with him, and he smiled confidently.

"This is when we must work together to take down the Pirates. We must try and take the Earthling's resources through peace like the Elders asked us to," he said carefully, weighing his words to make them sound as positive as possible. "We must all work together to support the greater cause instead of for individual glory. Let me remind you, my comrades, that we pledged to fall in battle together, but I will not lead you to failure. No. I will lead you to glory instead, and together, we will rise."

"Together, we will rise. Together, we will rise. Together, we will rise," they all chanted as Karl tried to hide his smile. He was glad he could at least manipulate his trodden-down crowd of soldiers.

"What blasted fools," he muttered an undertone as he watched them fall prey to his malign influence.

CHAPTER 8

PLOT OF ASSASSINATION

"What do you intend now, Captain?" Tatun asked, after hearing Karl rant about his ordeal regarding what he kept referring to as 'the Pirate Idiot.'

They were all inside the ship's battle room. An area lined with tables and chairs around a hexagon-shaped table set for five of his most trusted comrades. The lighting was dim to create an exclusive atmosphere. Karl felt it aided in freedom of speech. Unthreatened opinions were needed, and he didn't want to intimidate his followers yet. Tatun and Rye had requested a few day's off from their positions as the King's advisors due to what they were calling 'minor family concerns.'

In reality, the Captain said he wanted to pick their brains to solve his dilemma, but mostly, he wanted confirmation of his evil plans. He knew the rest of the Hermetites were too stubborn and disobedient to confide in such matters.

He would have had to painstakingly brainwash and control them, taking time, effort, and energy. But since the five were entirely under his manipulative control, they would not go against him. He knew they believed every word out of his mouth, and it certainly helped that Tatun and Rey were kin.

"What now?" Captain Karl echoed. "I don't know, what shall we do now? You, subordinate, is it not your duty to suggest some ideas? After all, what do I have you for?"

He was usually nicer to his bodyguards, but he was currently tense. Things almost always went his way, and he had been so sure that Tchaka would accept his invitation into an alliance. However, the unexpected refusal had set him back a few paces. It was not that he did not know what he should do. He just had too many alternate variables to consider.

"We could outright kill them?" Rye suggested. "We already have the weapons required to go to war."

The Captain pinched the area between his brows, frustration seeping into his tone as he said, "No. We can't. The Elders would never give us permission for that. If they find out we instigated war on any specie that did not attack us first, it would be going directly against their propaganda of peace.

The other thing is that we don't know how advanced the Pirates are. I've heard, from some sources, that they are primarily from a planet with a massive advocate for war. We don't know what weapons they might have as yet. We need to think about that also! Besides, our ammunition is limited to one war. I wouldn't want to run short of having to fight two battles simultaneously.

"If we eliminate the Pirates first, couldn't we confiscate their weapons?" One of the comrades asked.

The Captain replied, "Still, that would look bad to the powers that be. Much too aggressive."

"So, we intend to let them do whatever they want?"

"Definitely not!" Captain Karl snapped. "They need to vanish. They are not the kind of species we can allow to run around and do whatsoever. They would seriously cause harm to the planet, and I refuse to let them destroy the same planet I intend to rule. They can cause us problems if they interfere with our plans. They will surely give us problems if we don't interfere with theirs."

Captain Karl was more comfortable with Rye and Tatun than the rest of his subordinates because they were the only ones aware of his true intentions to rule over Earth. In his opinion, the others were all mindless pawns of the Panel of Elders.

"How about we wait and see what they will do?" Tatun asked. "They have already expressed a desire to kill the Earthling king. We can wait till they do invade the kingdom. Once they do so and establish control over the Earthling territory, we can wage war and eliminate them.

Captain Karl looked up, and his eyes were lit with delight. "You think I didn't think of that?" he demanded. He had not thought of that plan but would never admit it. A good assessment, he thought. But it was counterproductive to his objectives.

"I have, and that would be useless," he replied.

"How so, Captain?".

"For one, we can't let the Pirates take over because that would mean we could not do what the Elders demanded of us. We need resources. If we let the Pirates take over, they will destroy the resources the elders want to preserve. Second, suppose we intentionally allow a Pirate hostile takeover. In that case, there is a chance that the Elders will assume we no longer have control, and control is needed for a peaceful acquisition. This would surely cause a shutdown of the entire operation, leaving us with no support. I certainly don't want to war with the Elders just yet. They will think of it as a massive failure of us since a lower specie like the Pirates were able to take control. Not just that, the earthlings stand a better chance of destroying the Pirates than we do. And third," he said, finally confessing his real reason. "I want the Earthling King for myself. King Howard has disrespected me. I want to bring him down personally, and I refuse to let an inferior species take that lust away from me."

"Understood, Captain," Tatun said and stepped back.

He honestly did not want war. He had befriended some Earthlings and slowly realized they were not wrong. They had thrown their Captain out of the palace, but that was because they had a natural distrust against outsiders, mainly because they had to face many difficulties while trying to reestablish the kingdom.

It had not been easy recuperating from the last war that had almost destroyed them, leaving them barely able to build back out of the rubble and ash left behind. The Earthlings were a scarred but hardworking species, and he felt a certain amount of sympathy for them, despite everything Captain Karl had been saying.

"After that?" Rye asked.

"After they take care of the Pirates, we need to go on and dispose of the King. But first, we will manipulate the King into killing off the Pirates," Captain Karl said.

"How will we do that?" the question was asked.

"The boy. We have the King's nephew. I will use the boy to get the King's trust and slowly convince him to eliminate the Pirate species completely. I will make him believe that the Pirates threaten the Earthling peace, which they are, so I wouldn't even be lying about it. Then I shall head an army of purely Earthlings to defeat the Pirates. I will convince them that I have rescued the boy from the inhuman environment of the Pirates."

"But do you think the Earthlings will be able to conquer the Pirates if they are as strong as you have gauged?"

"Of course, they will. According to my information, the Earthlings have defeated the Pirates once, beaten them back to the shore, and burnt them down with fire, which is one of their weaknesses. The humans used flaming torches, which is something we do not have. We have laser and explosion technology instead of fire technology. It would be too time-consuming to train and equip our men with fire combat at this point. The Pirates have superior healing, except when hurt by fire, so our weapons won't be very effective against them."

"But won't the Pirates turn on us?" Rye asked.

"Fool!" Captain Karl spat, and Rye felt slight frustration creep up on him.

He had never felt wrong about the Captain demeaning him before, but living with the Earthlings opened his mind to accept their comparatively sensitive emotional range. He was not as sympathetic toward the Earthlings as his brother, but he honestly started believing in them. He learned they were an intricate, functioning, caring species.

"They will see me lead the Earthling army, but I will be disguised as one of them. I'm betting that Pirates are easily deceived. Pirates are not very intelligent species. They won't even suspect us while they are preoccupied with the locals. Besides, even if they do, they will be too busy fending off the Earthling army to try and attack us.

Even with their limited intelligence range, they know it would be unwise to instigate a new war while already engaged in another. I'm guessing they'd figure their chances of a victory would be diminished, being severally outnumbered and probably out-gunned as well," Karl explained.

"So, we will let the Earthlings wipe them out for us?" Tatun asked.

"Exactly, they've done it in the past." Captain Karl said triumphantly. "If there are any Pirate survivors, we will move in for the cleanup while they are weak."

He had devised the perfect plan on the spot and was very proud of himself. He could see it working, and he had already envisioned himself victorious. He saw himself at the head of an Earthling army, with his Hermetite forces safely out of harm's way. He couldn't wait to see Tchaka's head rolling on the ground, severed from the body, and stopping at his feet.

Captain Karl was not necessarily barbaric, but he could be ruthless, and he wished he could hang Tchaka's head on a pike on his wall as a reminder of the war. However, he knew that the Elders would find behavior like that extremely suspicious, so he would have to wait until he was the ruler of Earth. After that, he could do whatever he wanted.

"Take me to the boy," Captain Karl said. "He has been visually impaired, hasn't he? If I am going to 'rescue' him, I can't risk him identifying me."

"The boy's vision has been temporarily impaired while on the ship. Additionally, his hearing has also been altered," one of them said.

"Good," Captain Karl said, and the brothers' eyes widened in surprise.

It was the first time the Captain had approved of them. For a moment, they wondered if the Captain was losing his cruel touch but then realized that would be too good to be true. The Captain was a tough man, hardened by age, and he was not one to show any inclination of kindness.

Tchaka was halfway through gathering his army.

"It is time," he told Garnish, who looked slightly nervous.

"Are you sure?" Garnish asked. "I am hesitant about this entire thing. I think it was not very smart to send away the other species."

"You mean the Hermetites?" Tchaka asked.

Garnish nodded.

"They weren't going to help much anyway. They have their plans, and we have ours. I have waited years for this. The humans destroyed my father's people and burned his body beyond recognition. I will take my revenge."

"I thought you were excited about the Hermetite's presence?" Garnish asked. "I thought that was because you wanted to ally with them?"

"An alliance?" Tchaka demanded as if the word itself seemed too incredible to comprehend. "With those degenerate beggars who haven't even been here on Earth that long, and then to still think they are a superior specie? Nah, that will never happen."

"Then why-" Garnish began to ask, but Tchaka cut him off.

"Because we know the Earthling's true power. We know that they may seem like a weak species, but they have turned against us before, and they did that during a time when we had extreme amounts of power. They can turn against us again, but the Hermetites will not agree. As long as the Hermetites are around, the Earthlings will not be able to win against us. Half their forces will be too preoccupied trying to keep the Hermetites at bay while we storm in and take over."

"Take over?" Garnish asked.

"Honestly, I don't even want the Earthling King's throne. That's so pointless. I just want to torture the little weakling until he begs for mercy and then torture him some more. I want to kill his entire family before his eyes. I'll have fun with it," Tchaka said.

"Yeah, that sounds fun!" Garnish said in the local language, with a sarcastic tone.

He looked toward his soldiers practicing on the ship's blood-stained deck. They were all sparring against one another. They were using weapons to spar, but they believed in cultivating physical strength as a priority, which was why most of them had massive builds. They were short and stout, with stubby arms and legs and round barrel chests.

They constantly competed with one another to see who could have the strongest stomachs to deflect the most hits or who could belch the loudest, which always seemed to amuse them. It was their way of displaying pride in their war, with an apathetic nature.

Tchaka looked down at the sizable army he had gathered, and his heart swelled with pride. The Pirate's Black banner rose above their heads, with its traditional skull of death.

The Earthlings had no pennant flags or banners since they had never comprehended nor thought to declare sovereignty over any particular land. They saw all of the Earth as the people's entitlement. Territories were understood, and boundaries were respected. But these alien wars were a new concept.

Unlike the power struggles and interventions Howard encountered with the local villagers, these new wars would result in complete destruction.

The Pirate flag had a human skull, symbolizing the death and destruction Tchaka intended to inflict. He looked on, smiling when the flag fluttered in the wind.

Soon, it would be time to storm the Palace and kill the King. The man whose father and forefathers were responsible for the infernal death of his father, Sinkara. As he clenched his father's ring tight in his fist, he swore to his deceased, "I will avenge you."

CHAPTER 9

KNIGHT OF THE PALACE

"The child! Take me to the child!" Captain Karl demanded.

Rye winced at his harsh tone and nodded.

"As you wish," he said.

He and Tatun followed Captain Karl to the Fortress' brig, where they kept the little nephew captive.

Little Henry was an invaluable part of the invasion plan since he was the key through which Karl could gain the Earthling King's trust. He knew the plan had to quickly move forward because Tatun had informed him that the Earthling King, distraught with sorrow from losing his heir, was thinking of giving up his throne to the next in line and devoting all his time to finding the boy.

If that happened, Captain Karl would lose his leverage and have to rethink his master plan. He halted when they entered the chamber where Henry was being held.

"Why is it so infernally warm in here?" he questioned.

"Because Earthlings are hot-blooded," Rey explained, "They use fire to keep themselves warm. Otherwise, they get sick. We wouldn't want the little guy getting sick on us, so we only increased the temperature of this area,"

"Sick or not, We need to rough him up before I take him."

"Rough him up?" But, Captain, he is a mere child. Yes, he is of the Earthlings, one of the enemies, but he is still a child."

"If he goes back unscathed, do you think the King will believe that he was in any real danger in the first place? No, I need to make that King believe that I saved his nephew from the jaws of death. I must convince him that little Henry here would have died had I not risked my life to save him. That makes the story more credible, and I will be more likely to gain his trust," Captain Karl said.

He fiddled with some of his wristband controls, and two soldiers stumbled in.

"Go in and cover the child's eyes with a blindfold," he commanded, and they did as they were told.

Once his instructions had been followed, he dismissed his soldiers and entered the chamber with Tatun and Rye.

"Now," he said, altering his voice to make it more profound so that the little child would not recognize it. "Let the torture commence."

He punched the half-sleeping boy across the face, shaking him completely awake. Henry struggled from the shock of the hit when he found a blindfold obstructing his vision. His hands instinctively fled to his eyes, but before he could tug at the blindfold covering them, Captain Karl grabbed his hand, forced it on the ground, and stepped on his little fingers.

Henry howled in pain, and his blindfold dampened with tears. Tatun and Rye looked away, unable to stand the display of sadistic brutality.

"Let me go!" Henry yelled, letting out another blood-curdling scream that raised goosebumps on Rye's arms. However, both bodyguards remained silent, quiet disgust seeping from their prone figures. They knew that if they made a sound or spoke up to support Henry, Captain Karl would double the torture inflicted on the little boy.

Eventually, it all ended, leaving the boy with a bloody whimpering mess. At this time, Karl stepped out into the hallway, followed by his two minions.

"Drag him out of the ship and to the surface. We need to take him to his uncle," Captain Karl said in his dominant voice. His distraught bodyguards followed his commands but tried to treat the boy as gently as possible. They had never seen their Captain quite as brutal as this.

Captain Karl disguised himself as a member of the Earthling populace. He hid his pointy ears and changed into the regular Earthling clothes, cringing with extreme dissatisfaction when he saw how loosely the garments hung upon his body.

"Infernal clothing," he grumbled before leaving the ship. The boy, Tatun and Rye were already waiting for him on the surface.

"You may leave us. I will take the boy myself," Captain Karl said. He grasped the boy's shoulder. "We still need to alter his memories to make him think I saved him."

The two bodyguards nodded. They returned to the

Royal Palace to get ahead of Karl so that they would appear neutral. The Captain forced the sour pill between the boy's lips to alter any memory of the past few days. It would also leave him highly susceptible to anything he was told. Captain Karl would ultimately be in control of the boy's vulnerable state. A trick he had snuck on many of his disloyal followers in the past.

As soon as Henry swallowed the pill, he was knocked out briefly and awakened feeling confused. Captain Karl had already removed the blindfold from his eyes.

"Where am I? Who are you?" Henry asked.

"I am a warrior, a rogue fighter who saw your missing posters, little prince, and I saved you from the ruins of the South."

"The ruins of the South? When did I get here? Why don't I remember anything?"

He got up and winced in pain.

"Owww … How did I get all these bruises?" he wondered aloud.

"I believe you hit your head, little man, and lost your memories. The people in the South were in the act of torturing you. They had you tied up to a tree, and I risked my life to rescue you.

"Should I know you?" Henry asked.

"No, but I've heard a lot about you."

"Thank you for saving me, Sir!" Amazed by what the strange man was telling him. He saw the landscape and realized they were walking toward the palace. "Thank you for taking me home!"

"You're welcome, little prince. I hope you tell your King what happened,"

"Of course!" Henry said as they made their way toward the palace doors. All the locals in the village stopped to stare at the sight of the young prince with the stranger.

They had not seen him before. His dark hair and pale skin told them he was from an unknown land. They were slightly suspicious that he displayed his toes since most Earthlings did not possess sandals. A slight oversite of Karl, but still noticeable to the Earthlings. His complexion indicated that he must have dwelt in one of the underground colonies, away from the sun.

The guards opened the palace doors, and the two were led into a room lined with gold and silver. Pillers ordained with mythological heroes reaching up to the tall ceilings. Torches hung on the walls and lit the long walkway to the King's throne. The King stood to inquire why this stranger was entering without an announcement.

Suddenly, a little voice echoed in the room. "Uncle Howard!"

"Henry!" The King exclaimed when he saw the boy. He descended from his throne and rushed to embrace the boy. "Oh, how I missed you! Where have you been?"

"The South!" Henry said decidedly. "I was kidnapped and tortured by them. I probably wouldn't have survived if it wasn't for this kind-hearted warrior. I owe it to him. He saw me bound to a tree and risked his life to save me."

Henry did not recall any of this happening, but Captain Karl's glib charm, noble demeanor, and the way he carried himself with quiet and assured confidence made him believe that everything he had been told was true. In fact, Henry's active mind had even imagined how the entire scene had probably played out and was convinced that everything was true.

It was then that the King turned his attention to Captain Karl. Noticing the King's gaze on him, Captain Karl bowed graciously and got down on one knee as he'd seen done with others when seeking approval from the Earthling King.

"How fare thee, brave youth? I commend you for this brave deed."

"You are most welcome, your highness!"

King Howard then made a statement, being caught up in adrenalin. His excitement and gratitude were overwhelming.

"Arise, you are an esteemed guest. You don't have to bow before me," King Howard commanded. "As a reward for your noble service to us, I'll make you a part of my army, my special guard."

"You truly flatter me, your Highness," Captain Karl replied; then he stood up and winced, hissing as if he was in great pain, and clutched at his abdomen.

"What ails you?" King Howard asked, concerned.

"In the battle to free your nephew, I was wounded," Captain Karl lied. His face was such a perfect mask of pained innocence. His handsome features, coupled with the air of nobility he exuded, would have made even the sharpest man believe what he was trying to portray.

King Howard found no reason to doubt him. In fact, he was more concerned that his savior was hurt.

"Ah, my good man! Excuse my thoughtlessness. Here I am prattling on about making you part of my army, but you require rest and food. Thank you for returning my heir. I assure you that you will be subjected to the best treatment my men can offer, and you will want for nothing while you are with us."

"*While You're with us*?" Karl echoed in his head. A little glitch in the plan he hadn't figured on, although staying inside the Palace might be an asset.

"I thank you, King Howard," Captain Karl said.

"But first, dear man, tell me who you are," the King called out before Karl could walk away.

"I am a rogue fighter, your highness. I go by the name Everwell. I was born in an Earthling colony, one of the very few that chose to exist independently of your reign, and because of that, my territory is dying. I have long been in search of your lands.

Howard looked down at his nephew with a kind heart.

"Praise God that got you here," he replied. "Guards, clean him up before you take him to his mother, and please, sir Everwell, tell us of your rescue."

"While on my journey, I saw a boy tied to a tree, seemingly left to die, and since he was a mere lad, I couldn't allow myself to look on. No one should deserve that kind of treatment, regardless of the crime. Unfortunately, I was injured during the fight and had to flee from the pirates that came out of nowhere. They were a fighting bunch, but I was able to escape. Let's say luck was on my side.

I shudder to think what their intentions were for the boy. Later I recognized him from the posters."

"You're a courageous man," King Howard began. "Remind me to thank our artists for the rendering of Henry on the posters. It was a job well done."

"My sire, I merely look upon opportunities as they come and take them when they do," Captain Karl explained, bowing humbly once more with another dramatic wince of exaggerated pain.

Tatun and Rye, who had reached the palace before Karl, had slipped into the hall and managed to stand parallel to the King's throne at attention, ready for any royal commands.

"Sire, we have researched what has been shared. He speaks the truth," Rye said. "Your nephew's words alone are proof enough."

"Take Henry to his mother," the King said, and Tatun took Henry out of the hall.

"Brave youth, Everwell," the King addressed the strange visitor again. "You have done me a great deed. Everwell, you must be appointed as part of my army. But first," He said, "You must rest."

Captain Karl nodded. His expression was meek, like that of an exhausted man.

"Rye, take him to the best guest chambers in the palace and ensure he is given the treatment he requires."

Rye did as he was bid. He led Captain Karl away from the throne room and then followed him with some restraint. As soon as they were in the hall together, Captain Karl abandoned all pretenses.

"The guest chambers?" he scoffed, keeping his voice low in case he was heard. "Soon enough, I will kill that old man and take his chambers and throne for myself."

Rye glanced at his Captain and felt a sudden wave of extreme anger wash over him. He knew he was indebted to Captain Karl for raising him, but he couldn't help but also feel terrified of how sadistic the Captain was. They had advocated peace, and their entire species was peace-loving, but Captain Karl was not one of them.

He was a Hermetite, yet power had corrupted him so drastically that he had reduced himself to torturing a mere child for selfish motives. Now, for the first time, Rye wondered how someone so fair-faced and with such polished manners could have such a rotten core.

Still, he quelled his anger and led Captain Karl to his chambers, knowing that the faster everything was over, the faster he could escape the detestable Captain's company. Doubts had sprung up within him, causing this sudden realization. He no longer wanted any part of the Captain's evil plan to rule Earth.

"Captain, are you sure you want this?" he asked as soon as they were alone in the room. "This torture, pain, and destruction is not how we do things."

"Are you questioning me?" Captain Karl thundered, his voice vibrating with barely restrained anger. "The one who raised you and ensured you had a home? I am the one who gave you a place and a purpose. Are you questioning everything I have done for you?"

"Of course not, Captain," Rye protested. "I just think that torturing the child was going too far."

"Have you gone soft?" Captain Karl scoffed. "If you have, you may offer yourself a Hermatite sacrifice, for I would no longer need you."

"Captain, I just believe that we may work this out through peace. There is no reason to harm the Earthlings or plan their destruction."

"You will not ruin my plan now," Captain Karl threatened him, realizing that Rye must have had a change of heart. "You have stood by me obediently for years, and now you change? Has your alliance weakened? You will obey me until I no longer need you. Do you not remember your training? You were raised to be commanded by me. Do you understand?"

"Yes," Rye said dejectedly.

"Yes, what?" Captain Karl demanded.

"Yes, King Karl," Rye said, and Captain smiled like the cat that had gotten the cream.

He had instructed his two loyal subordinates, Rye and Tatun, to address him as 'King' when they were alone, and he was pleased to see that his rules were being followed.

"Now, you will convince Howard to enlist me as Commander of the King's guards. And if you cannot do that, you must at least make me an assistant to the guard. Do you understand me?" Captain Karl asked.

"Yes, my King," Rye said bitterly.

"Excellent. Dismissed," Captain Karl said, and Rye left the room.

Rye found King Howard already in the process of sending for his advisors. When all the advisors gathered, there was a meeting.

"We need to show our gratitude to the young man. Everwell saved my nephew, risking his own life, and I owe him a position in the army. I believe he can tremendously benefit us, and want to keep him. What do all of you suggest?"

"I agree," Rye called out, and the other advisors murmured, approving the decision.

"I believe that we should make him the King's Guard and the main commander of his forces," Tatun said. Suddenly, silence reigned the hall.

"I am not sure if the current heads of the commandeer would be happy with that," the King said.

"But he is right," one of the more foolish advisors commented. "He is a rouge fighter. He could know techniques that our forces may not, which probably played a role in his encounter with Henery's pursuing Pirates."

"If not the army commander, he can be made the advisor to the commander and the main strategist," Rye suggested hopefully.

He wanted everything to be over with because the sooner Karl's diabolical plan was secured, the sooner he could be out of the Captain's control. Once Captain Karl was Earth's ruler, Rye would return to Hermes.

He no longer wanted to be one of Captain Karl's puppets. He did not know how Tatun felt about it but was counting on his brother's concurrence.

"Commander!" Howard shouted, "He shall be made commander of my military. He will lead my army into war!" King Howard declared, and Tatun and Rye sighed while the rest of the advisors cheered.

He instructed his Guard to switch, and the decision was finalized.

The two Hermetite brothers looked at each other. King Howard's decision was like a hammer being hit against an anvil - without even knowing it, King Howard had made a decision that inevitably brought them closer to the ultimate destruction and ruination of the Earthling specie. The King was secretly criticized for his irrational, spontaneous decision-making, but his authority was never questioned.

Fortunately for Karl, the King did not thoroughly research his background before ordering their fate. Taking men at face value was the King's only downfall, and the Captain knew it. Karl learned this about the Earthling King through his encounter with him and his associate, Aster, many years ago.

CHAPTER 10

PLOTTING

Captain Karl looked around at the room he was in. The furnishings were mainly wooden, homely, and warm. The color themes were primarily red and gold, with brass copper plating on the window sills. Nothing was to his taste.

He scrunched his nose with disgust, hating the sight of the coarsely made furniture around him.

"Fit for a King?" he scoffed. "Fit for an Earthling King, but definitely not a Hermetite one. When I am King, all this shall be remade from metal and glass. None of these peasant furnishings are fit for someone like me."

He had closely observed the King's guards and the men. King Howard had one solitary guard because he thought he was in no danger. The military and the rest of the men were situated inside the palace, so if need be, the King could be easily protected at all times.

The guard could quickly be taken care of, but harming the guard or the King would be like stepping foot into a lion's den and provoking it, especially since they were surrounded by the King's forces on all sides.

There was a knock on the door. Captain Karl picked up an ornate, gold-plated candle stand and inspected it.

"Come in," he stated, barely looking at the entrance.

The doors opened, and two of the King's guards, along with Tatun, stepped into the room. The captain set down the candle stand and turned to look at them, one eyebrow raised in question.

"Is everything okay?" he asked, looking princely, even in his shoddy robes. He had not been provided a good change of clothes and was waiting for them.

"Of course," Tatun said. "The King requests your presence when you are ready, Mister Everwell. He has news for you."

"Is something the matter?" the captain asked, feigning concern.

He really did not care because the worst that the Earthlings could do was throw him out, and they had already done that once. Besides, he had saved the King's nephew and was sure the King would not treat him poorly.

"Nothing at all," Tatun said. "It is positive news. The King has also sent garments for you to dress in and some attendants to run your bath."

Two attendants stood out from the little party and stepped toward Everwell, waiting for his word.

"I would like that," he told them, and immediately, they made their way to the bathing chamber and got busy cooling the water, ensuring it was cooled sufficiently enough for a

Hermetilte and adding the fragrant washing oils available at his disposal.

The two guards then stepped forward and presented the captain with some robes, which he graciously took with a graceful bow of thanks. Then they all stepped back, waiting for his permission to leave.

"Is that all you require, Everwell?" Tatun asked, trying hard to hide his grin when he saw the captain scowl at the new name. He was also amused at the chance to address the captain without any of his official or unofficial titles. It was not a name of his own choosing, but it had been an excellent human name that would stand out, and Captain Karl was aware that he needed to stand out, especially if he was going to be the King's guard.

"Yes, dismissed," Captain Karl said in carefully clipped tones, and then he was alone again.

He bathed, dressed, and then rested on the bed. Nothing about the place impressed him, and he wondered how the Earthlings thought this was the lap of luxury. In fact, the Earthling dwellings made him feel extremely uncomfortable. The small window let very little light into the room and was shaded to cut even more light. The bath water had been too warm, suited only for Earthling body temperature. The weather was too humid, the clothes were too loose, and the scented bath oils were foul.

He found fault with everything and realized how much he would change once he was King.

Eventually, he made his way outside. As he left the chamber, the stationed guards immediately fell into place beside him, ready to escort him to the King. An act which begrudgingly impressed him.

'My subordinates, too, must be made this obedient,' he mused silently.

The guards escorted him to the King's dining room, where Howard was already waiting. A magnificent feast was spread before them on a table set for at least fifty. He had never dined with Earthlings before and was concerned about conversing with so many and blowing his cover. Going incognito was easy for him, but it could be a problem if caught off guard by some persistent inquisitive onlooker. Luckily he was invited to sit with the King.

"I hope I have not inconvenienced you in any way," Karl said politely.

"Not at all," the King replied gaily. "You saved my dear nephew. The very least I can offer you is a kind welcome and a place in my military force."

"The military force?" Karl asked, pretending to be shocked. "That is such a huge honor. I could never accept that!"

"Oh, you must," the King insisted. "What is more, my good man, you will be made head of the forces. I can barely imagine the many men you had to fight to save Henry at such risk to your own life. You have proven yourself to be a strong warrior of the highest caliber, and as such, you've earned this place at the top."

"But what about the current head of your guards? Won't he be demoted? Will that be fair to him?" Karl asked, feigning concern.

"Of course not. He has been made one of my advisors. He has served me faithfully for many long years. He is not as hearty as you, young Everwell. He is wizened and capable enough to be a worthy advisor to me."

"I thank ye, good King, for the honor you have bestowed upon me. I shall try my very best to live up to your expectations."

"A toast to the brave man who saved my Nephew from death. You are a brave and honest man Everwell. I'm confident you'll be honed in your duties. You can count on my support for anything."

A short feeling of solace welled inside him but disappeared as quickly as it came. He wanted out of the room but knew his duties were to be accepted into the King's service and were also crucial to his plan.

When Karl was instated as the head of the army, he kept his eyes and ears open. He realized, soon enough, that the Earthling army was much larger than he had thought it was. The palace had massive walls and a fortress-like surrounding structure to keep out uninvited visitors or enemy forces. The enclosed field was constantly being utilized for battle training. Weapon storage was a building as big as the King's dining room with a lock as big as a megalith stone securing a massive entrance door. It required two men to unlock, remove it and open it..

The army was widespread, and the King had his spies spread throughout. Although the King was somewhat gullible and modestly intelligent enough to know, there would always be a rouge warrior attempting to challenge the system. He had his processes in place to stifle any internal malicious uprising.

He needed the confidence of his Head of operations. Naïvely handing over complete control to a man he barely knew, yet felt strongly compelled to do so, made perfect sense to Howard. The King thought he had always been a good judge of character and Everwell was a savior. A compassionate man who thought of others over himself couldn't be wrong. "Shoot now, ask questions later" had never been Howard's way, but his exuberance at Henery's return seemed to obstruct his rationality.

Karl's hypnotic nature was starting to pay off.

It wasn't long before Karl noticed that the King's forces were well-structured and prepared. They were reasonably good at offense, but their defense was top-notch. They were accustomed to fending off external attacks from menacing Pirates. Since the war at sea allowed them to reverse engineer abandoned Piratoon's weaponry, the Earthlings were now a force to be reckoned with.

They also knew the terrain the Hermetites did not, which would benefit the royal army, giving them an advantage.

He inspected the training methods used by the Earthling forces and realized that they were well-skilled at hand-to-hand combat and pre-judging long-distance weapon accuracy. The majority of the Hermetite weaponry required closer proximity to be successful. This would be another clear Hermetite disadvantage. The more the Captain saw, the more uneasy he became, so Karl's internal plan was the only way to win.

'It is a foolproof plan,' he thought.

It was becoming more apparent that he underestimated the Earthling forces. They had strong bonds that Karl knew would be hard to break. In the case of a head-on assault, they would split up and attack their foe from all sides. It was a strategic maneuver they called *'divide and conquer.'*

Several days later, he called a meeting at the Fortress.

"Trusted allies, I have spent enough time with the armies of this planet and have alarming details that we need to be aware of.. Their forces are stronger than we thought, and we will inevitably face casualties. The King's men use poisonous arrowheads. The arrowheads were designed to spin, penetrate, and lock into their victim. If the shot struck bone, it could not easily be removed due to the barbed tips, allowing more time for the poison to enter the body and slowly kill them, providing that the painstaking removal process didn't kill them first. Unfortunately, the odds of a victim's survival were slim. All of them are not only skilled archers, but they are also good swordsmen. Since most of our weapons are close-range, swordsmen are easy to take care of, but our laser technology uses a compound of gamma and beta rays that may not travel as far as their arrows," the Captain told them, pacing his chambers.

"Captain, how about we-" Tatun began, but the Captain turned on him and glared.

"What did you call me?" he demanded.

"Captain?" Tatun asked, confused.

"And what have I asked you to call me when we are in private?" the Captain clamored.

"Sire," Tatun said with a slight wince, his eyes widening in realization. "Sire. Of course, I apologize."

"Now," Captain Karl continued smugly. "What were you suggesting?"

"Need we attack the Earthling forces at all? They have done well for themselves, and they are not as Terri-," Tatun began to say, but Rye pinched his arm, and immediately, he was forced to change his words. "Yes, of course. We will provide any solutions to take down the Earthling forces. We stand beside you at all times."

The Captain was too preoccupied to pay attention to his bodyguard's opinions. They were mere pawns to him, but he always heard them when they'd verified his ideas. Being intelligent and brilliant was futile if nobody was around to admire him for it, and he liked it when his little minions looked at him in awe as if he was the cleverest Hermetite.

"Of course. Of course," the Captain said mindlessly. "But my idea is better. Now listen to this. Since we can not attack from the outside, we must attack from the inside. We have made it here, into the enemy forces, got our way to the top, and manipulated the king into trusting us. All this was done because of my planning. I have singlehandedly carried us thus far, and I can take us further. Instead of controlling the Earthling army, we can cause it to fold in. They will fall once we convince them to fight amongst themselves. We need not intervene until their army is on the verge of collapse, and then the Hermetites can step in and take control."

The Captain paused, waiting for one of his minions to eagerly deliver him the praise he expected.

"Excellent idea, sire," Rye said with the slightest eye roll. "How exactly do you plan to do this?"

"Good question," the Captain said, a bright smile covering his face. "This is precisely the reason why I keep you around."

Tatun covered up his condescending scoff with a cough, which the Captain barely noticed.

"Now, we send word to our forces, telling them that the army is so big it requires mutiny to rattle its foundations. Once that is done, we can figure out how to cause such a mutiny. I will need one of you to visit the Fortress and inform my people about my intentions. Make sure to show me in as favorable a light as possible since I require the Hermetites to not suspect that I am the one behind the war. They need to think the Earthlings themselves did so."

"Why can't we tell the others?" Tatun wondered.

"Foolish, pawn. Do you not realize that if there are spies from the Elders amongst us, my power will be taken from me before the mid-day sun falls to the horizon?" Captain Karl exclaimed.

"Yes, sire," Tatun said complacently.

"Rye," the Captain said. "You will be informing my forces of the proceedings. I cannot trust this treasonable moron to carry out any task adequately."

Tatun winced, hiding his scowl. He was tired of Captain

Karl's attitude. There was no need for him to be rude, and Tatun compared-him with the actions of the Earthling King, who had been kind to him and his brother since they had been accepted into his circle.

'The Earthling king is a true king in every aspect of the word,' Rye mused, hating that he should be tasked with fooling the Hermetite forces, making them believe Captain Karl was doing everything for the greater good.

"Back home, I would surely be accused of treason," He thought. *"I would have some serious explaining to do. In my own defense, I must say that I was tricked."*

"What do I tell our own forces?" Rye asked.

"Tell them," the Captain said thoughtfully.

"To hold off the attack since the Earthling forces are worse than I had thought. Emphasize the Earthlings' brutality, and tell them that the King is an old fool who finds amusement in war. Make the Earthlings seem like a terrible species that must be destroyed at all costs to save Earth. Lastly, inform them we are holding off the attack because I intend to make their forces turn against each other since that would be the wisest approach."

"Noted, Sire," Rye said with a nod. "What will Tatun be doing?"

Captain Karl scoffed.

"That is for me to decide. You are dismissed. Leave," Karl commanded.

Rye left, hiding the scowl on his face. He had begun to truly hate the man who claimed to raise him.

"Now, you clumsy pawn," the Captain said, addressing

Tatun, unsuspecting of the real measure of mistrust he had already installed in him. "You and I must assess the populace. We must look for influential individuals to convince us to start a rebellion. We must narrow down our candidates and pick someone sufficiently influential so that enough Earthlings will be tempted to follow him and rise against the Earthling King."

The Captain grinned in a manner that made Tatun cringe. Things were about to get ugly for the Earthlings, and Tatun hoped they would be victorious. They were a peaceful population, and he wholeheartedly believed they deserved to live and prosper peacefully on their own entitled planet.

CHAPTER 11

THE REBELLION

Captain Karl had been scouting the Earthling's forces and had narrowed down the people he could select to start a mutiny. The more he lived with their specie, the more disgusted he became by everything around him.

Their food was too well-spiced and soft instead of the tough, bland vegetables he was used to. Their clothing was too ugly since the garments were generally supposed to be loose-fitting instead of the tights the Hermetites were used to wearing. He hated the place and wanted to do his best to get out of there as soon as possible.

That was why, instead of having his minions do things, he had quickly stepped in to lend a hand. One thing he had done was summon some of his trusted men from the Fortress. He had to be strategic with that because he knew that the Hermetites, also obedient to him, were genuinely loyal to the Elders.

Those forces had been supplied to him by the Elders, and he was entirely sure that some of them were the Elders' spies. Therefore, he needed to handpick the ones he knew were on his side. Tatun and Ry were easy since they would do whatever he told them. He had their undying loyalty, or so he thought.

In the same way, Karl had also started cherry-picking some Earthling warriors to do his bidding since it was too tricky

for Hermetites to tolerate the warm, moist Earthling atmosphere. He had no idea how they survived without Artificial Temperature Controls like the kind that were back on the ship because the season's heat was unbearable to him. He would have to wait for cooler days to take any action.

His men, on the whole, had managed to find five suitable candidates. One of them was Cartella Briar. She was one of the best warriors that the king had, and he had found out that if he had not stepped in, she would have been the one who was going to be the next head of the King's guards.

Captain Karl had thought about approaching her, but he decided to watch her from a distance for a short while, keeping out of sight yet close enough to overhear conversations with associates and realized she was not someone who would be easily manipulated to start a mutiny.

She was uninterested in the political mindset, and being the Head of the King's Guard was not an inspiration for her. Although being rouge-ish was admirable, her strong will and convictions were not to Karl's liking. She seemed too much like himself, and he certainly didn't need another ego to deal with.

The next candidate had been one of the King's advisors.

But when evaluated, he proved much too loyal to the king. Another person who was high on the candidate list was Aster.

The king trusted Aster, and Karl initially thought he could manipulate Aster like he had manipulated the King by gaining his trust through his chivalry in saving the King's nephew. He once held a long conversation with Aster during one of the meetings the king had called, detailing the multiple wounds he received during the rescue.

Although Aster knew his own species, he was not convinced that Karl was not a Hermetite supporter. He was generally very distrustful of him. He believed that Cartella Briar should be the Head of the King's Guards because, in his words, "Those who understand the weight of power never really covet it and are less likely to abuse it."

The fourth candidate was Isabella Stolla Enza. She was the oldest, and her dark hair had already faded to a salt and pepper shade. The edges of her eyes were wrinkled with wisdom, and her eyes were marked with laugh lines.

Isabella was once the King's most excellent strategist and feared warrior. Some people hoped Cartella would walk in her footsteps. Isabella had been held in high regard in the king's court and had no enemies other than the men she bested in battle. She was petite, yet her swift talent gave her an edge over most opponents. All of her comrades adored her for her sophisticated and robust character.

She devised the battle strategy that ultimately led the Pirates back to the sea and met their downfall in the historic battle of the Sea. Even at her older age, her movements were agile and swift, albeit full of grace. She had briefly been the Head of the King's Guard. But, not finding the position to her taste, she soon decided to retire and devote herself to Botany. An interest she established in childhood.

Apart from being a great warrior, she was a healer who people often sought out. From headaches to poisoned wounds, she had a cure for everything. Since a young age, she has been able to accurately predict the weather.

If he managed to convince her, Karl thought, she would be able to convince the masses of people who blindly trusted her to follow him. But he overlooked her simply because she had already resigned, and he was not keen on including the strong dominant type in his company, capable of overtaking even his own followers. He knew she would surely be harder to control.

Lastly, the one candidate he had set his sights upon was Victor Abernum.

Victor was strong, quick on his feet, and an excellent fighter. Personally, Karl had observed Victor in battle and had to admit that he was slightly better than all the rest, but he was certainly not the best.

Besides, he had yet to beat Cartella Briar.

Apart from that, his aim with a bow and arrow was impeccable, and his specialty was hitting moving targets. Captain Karl had seen him in action and had been severely impressed by Victor's agility with a bow, but that was not the only reason Victor would be a brilliant candidate.

Much like Karl, he had an overbearing, controlling personality and could easily create syntax for his beliefs, pulling the wool over the eyes of the ignorant. Karl admired such qualities in a man.

He was a man who had great ambition. In fact, he had been after the Head of the King's Guards position and hated Karl for getting it. He had already secured a place by bribing seven of the King's eleven advisors to elect him for the next reign.

However, when Karl was given the position, Victor lost his temper and went on a mad rampage. He had lost much money, time, and effort trying to convince the advisors, and he did not appreciate all his efforts going down the drain.

Apart from that, he was very persistent and outgoing. He frequently visited inns and drank barrels of local mead, striking up business connections, and was usually well-liked because of how hearty he was. He had gardened an ardent fan following over the years, and many of the local populace, who had never seen him in battle, were convinced through many of Victor's drunken announcements that he was one of the greatest warriors, second only to Isabella.

All of them were very disappointed when King Howard chose Everwell, the stranger, instead of Victor. However, King Howard was not inclined toward Victor, and everyone knew that.

The king believed that Victor was the kind of man who was too ambitious and had the potential to abuse any power granted to him. The king was right because, apart from being charismatic, strong, and well-loved, Victor was also a selfish glutton with greed for monetary wealth, known to be moody at times. Probably brought on by a hangover from his nights at the inn.

He did not have many desires in life, but he loved the idea of squandering them away on women and cheap booze. He was a notorious rake, perhaps why almost every subject, including Aster, distrusted him.

They believed he was too immoral and unserious to hold any military position for long, but he had proved them wrong thus far by spending almost two decades as a king's soldier.

Captain Karl stood at the tower battlements and watched from where he got a bird's eye view of everything. He saw his guards approach Victor informing him of the meeting Karl wished to have with him.

He could not hear the conversation from that far, but he could tell Victor was reluctant to be summoned.

Soon enough, a while later, the door to the battlements was thrown open, and Victor entered, trailed by the two guards who responsibly escorted him.

"We have brought him, Master Everwell," they said.

Karl nodded, wincing at the title. He still had not gotten used to it. For some reason, even though he had been the one who had chosen it, he had grown to hate this fake 'Earthling' name.

"Dismissed," Karl said, keeping his gaze fixed on Victor, and the guards left, shutting the doors behind him.

"What do you want?" Victor demanded, crossing his arms over his chest. Karl had been right. Victor hated him and wanted nothing to do with him.

"It's not about what I want," Karl said confidently, nodding to dominate their exchange. "It's about what you want."

"What do I want?" Victor scoffed. "And why would that matter to you?"

"Because we have mutual tastes," Karl said. "And yet we want opposite things. You want my position as the Head of the King's Guards, and I want to give it up."

Victor's eyes widened.

"What are you talking about?" he demanded.

"Look, Victor. Let's be honest here. You want my position, and I want to give it up. So you can have it," Karl said.

Victor tilted his head to one side, narrowing his eyes suspiciously.

"And what's the catch here? You want nothing in return for it?" he asked.

Captain Karl laughed.

"Not nothing!" he emphasized. "But not what you think I want. Unlike you, I do not desire wealth, fame, or grandeur. I wish to be able to leave. I was not given this position willingly since I thought I would be able to leave once I handed little Henry over to the King. He insisted that I was the best candidate for the Head of the Guards, and so, I was forced into keeping the position bestowed upon me, and I cannot leave until I have served ten harvests here."

"Why don't you want the position?" Victor argued.

"Because I am a wanderer and a rogue traveler. Your kingdom has too many rules and formal practices. I wish to have the freedom I had before, but I can't leave so soon," Karl lied.

"That is an interesting sob story, but what do you want me to do about it?" Victor asked.

"Start a rebellion against the King!" Karl declared, and Victor's mouth dropped open. He took a few shocked steps backward and then righted himself.

"A rebellion against King Howard? Are you hearing yourself? You're asking me to start mutiny!" Victor said, his voice raised.

"Well then, what other option do we have? I will stay stuck here for ten harvests, and you will never get this position," Karl said.

"Never?" Victor asked. "I'll get it after you leave."

Karl shook his head, "Are you willing to wait that long? Did you know that the King prefers Isabella over you? Even after I leave, she'll be the next pick. So, regardless of however many advisors you bribe, at the end of the day, the king holds the ultimate power."

"How?" Victor asked. "How do you know that I bribe anyone?"

"Because I have eyes and ears everywhere."

"Hmph!" Victor nodded while staring at the wood-planked floor, trying to remember.

"I have never paid for support, nor have I given away for privacy!" he snarled after musing on it. "But there is still a chance the King could make me his head. You can make a mistake in your judgment and be replaced."

"Trust me. In one of our meetings, he called you a

pompous fool without enough brains to string together two sentences. We're a lot alike, Victor. I am a good judge of character, and I believe you're the man to lead over me. I also believe your right for this kingdom," Karl lied.

Victor gritted his teeth and let out a string of utterly blasphemous expletives.

"How dare he?" Victor demanded, and Karl grinned.

Anger meant that Victor was no longer thinking clearly. Karl knew that anger and love were two emotions that could drive men mad, and he was not above taking advantage of both.

"So that's why you won't be head of guards, even after me. I want my freedom, and you want this position. Besides, you have enough followers, and it would be easy to convince them since they all admire and respect you.

Apart from that, I have also found out that many of the population are skeptical about the King's decision to pass on the crown to his heir. Even though he is young, his nephew is still blood. Family inheritance is the usual tradition unless the family member is compromised somehow.

Even Isabella, the great strategist, is firmly opposed to a boy King since he will need financial and military consultants. With you at the helm, Victor, you'd be in total control of the entire kingdom."

"That's true," Victor said, nodding and agreeing with Karl. "Now that you put it that way, mutiny is the only way." Pacing across the floor, he silently debated his thoughts to himself.

"I must remove the King," he kept chanting.

'This is my calling,' he thought, *'It's finally come down to putting my money where my mouth is.'*

"So, here is what we can do!" Victor exclaimed, exercising his controlling persona needed for the task. "In the next few days, I will send my men to all the surrounding villages and nail postscripts to doors, trees, and the like, telling them why allowing Henry to be the new boy king would be preposterous. This will take time, but it is doable."

"Excellent idea. Mutiny is a good plan," Karl said, pretending the entire thing was Victor's idea. By staying in the background, he could still pull the strings.

'Victor will make an excellent puppet,' he thought to himself.

"Yes," Victor nodded. "Next, we will start holding demonstrations, and finally, while the King is overwhelmed with the local farming population's rebellions, I will focus on turning his military against him."

"That ... wow. I'm speechless," Karl encouraged. "You're brilliant."

"Even if the boy did somehow manage to become King, I will occupy the seat of military control and be the King's right hand," Victor thought out loud.

"That's how I see it. It's a win-win for both of us." Karl remarked.

He wanted to roll his eyes but refrained from it and tried not to cringe at his words.

"Thank you," Victor said. "While I do all that, you can gain the King's trust and make sure he is hindered in every way possible."

"I'll do that," Karl lied. He intended to do no such thing. He had already planted the seed and knew it would come to fruition without his assistance. He knew that the fewer people he involved in his scheme, the less likely the plan would backfire.

"Right. I'll go to the bar now. It might take time, but it might be doable. Give me two moons to spread the word," Victor said, backing away.

"Noted," Karl said.

Karl watched as Victor left the battlements and then laughed in sheer satisfaction. Over the next few days, the movement spread. The groups gained power, and a sizable number of people rebelled against the king.

"I like Victor," Karl thought. "He's my kind of guy."

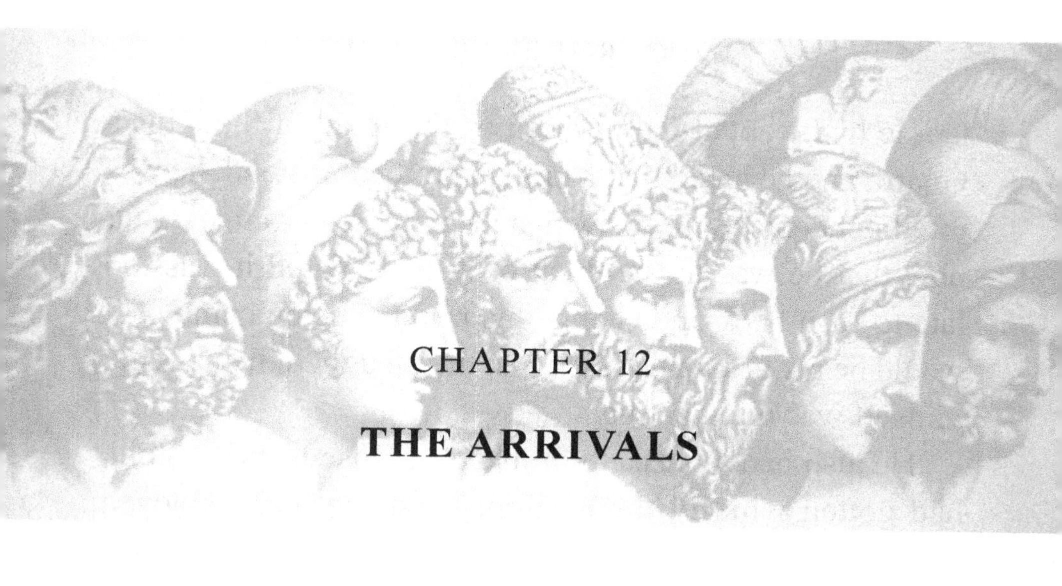

CHAPTER 12

THE ARRIVALS

Victor's movement gained extreme power, and the rebellion expanded over the region quickly. Victor had convinced people to stand up against the king and start a mutiny against King Howard. The petty reasons he provided made sense and hurt enough sentiments to warrant an uprising.

He was silver-tongued enough to convince the weaker followers. It turns out Victor was a competent candidate for Karl. Karl was delighted with the preparations. It was all going as planned.

On the other hand, Victor was having a change of heart. He was not the kind of person who planned mutinies. He had agreed to help Karl out of some sense of twisted hatred, he suspected, toward the King. Since anyone would surely want that position, why wouldn't Everwell?

The more he thought about it, the more he realized that he was not necessarily inclined to engage in any revenge of a newcomer. Especially someone rejecting such a prestigious position offered to him.

He had wanted the position as the Head of the King's Guard, and he hated that Karl had gotten it instead; he was intelligent enough to know that something was amiss. But, now that he was in the thick of it, he realized it was too late to turn back and change his mind. The outcome of it would be rewarding enough. Just the thought of being King himself was intoxicating.

He also had a pressing problem because Isabella Stolla had gotten wind of the situation, and she had employed Cartella Briar to raise an opposing force to counter Victor's mutinous crew.

Once the King heard what was happening behind his back, he immediately asked Isabella for advice.

Even though she was not his wife, in many ways, she was the queen piece of his kingdom. She was the advisor he turned to when he needed complete guidance. In contrast, Aster was still his rook, head of the guard, and a trusted comrade.

Howard wondered how things had gotten so messed up. As Aster had pointed out, everything seemed to have gone amiss after the arrival of Henry's rescuer. Howard had seen the darkness hiding behind Everwell's face, yet he still decided to give him a chance, hoping he would do well. After all, he still thought that he had been the one that saved his nephew. Alas, he had been betrayed and was unaware of it.

While Victor's group was on the rise, Cartella started to work on convincing the movement to die down. She challenged Victor's mutinous and their enthusiasm with logical sense.

Her method worked, but at one point, the two forces, Cartella's and Victor's, came to a standstill. Many days had passed, and the kingdom was starting to divide; those who stood beside the King and those who stood against him. By the end of the season, the trade routes dramatically decreased from the fear of an invasion by opposing forces. It got so severe that Cartella formally proposed a one-on-one meeting with Victor.

Victor, also covertly weary of the war, agreed and met a few days later.

"Soldier," Cartella greeted him with a nod. They were in the same position, but she preferred to address people by their rank instead of their names.

"Come, Cartella, we've fought in many wars together. There is no need to be so formal. Call me Victor," he said.

Cartella gritted her teeth and said, "In case you haven't noticed, we're on opposing sides right now, and it's not the ideal situation to be friendly with, Victor."

She spat out his name like it was contaminated.

"Look, come over to our side. It's fun. We can get the King off his throne and use his wealth to drink and dance to our heart's content."

"Dance to your heart's content?" she scowled, disgusted. "Drink yourself to death, by all means. Just don't pull the kingdom and its people down with you. I don't even understand why you're doing this!"

Victor took a step closer and lifted her chin with one slender finger, making her grimace deepen.

"Why am I doing this? Maybe it has something to do with you constantly being better than me?" he asked.

"Does it?" she asked. "Or does it have everything to do with your egoistical ambition?"

"I wouldn't be this covetous if you weren't so greedy and intent on outperforming me in everything!" he yelled, stepping back and running his fingers through his hair. "You've done this since we were kids, and I am tired of it!"

"Outperforming?" Cartella asked, and suddenly, an idea struck her. Victor was smart, but Cartella was smarter. Victor could move men and the masses with his tongue, but Cartella could sweetly lie into moving hearts and change intentions.

She had that kind of power over most men due to her stunning good looks and persuasiveness.

"Yes. Isn't that what you've been trying to do all this time?" he asked.

Cartella stepped closer to him and sighed, her expression softening almost immediately.

"I was never outperforming you. I always tried to be as good as you so that I could keep up. So that you wouldn't leave me behind and forget all about me!" she declared.

His eyes widened in shock, and he turned to her.

"Wha-What?" he asked.

She moved closer to him and raised herself on her tiptoes so that her breath caressed his skin when she spoke.

"I've always been in love with you," she whispered. "Didn't you know that?"

Victor almost turned away, unsure how to feel about it, but at the end moment, he stopped and looked into her honest eyes.

"I didn't," Victor said. "And why? Why are you telling me this now?"

"Because it hurts me, Victor," Cartella sighed. "It hurts to see you so constantly stressed. Join me. Join us, and I will ensure the king favors you beyond belief. I have never wanted any positions, and I know you covet the position of the Head of Guards. Let go of this greed, Victor. Please. Let go."

She placed a featherlight kiss on his lips and drew away before he had the time to react.

"Please," she murmured one last time and then left the area.

Victor stood there, staring at the door she had disappeared through, trying to wrap his head around everything. He and Cartella had once been childhood friends, and then they had both changed and drifted away. He smiled at the thought that she harbored feelings for him because he had once harbored feelings for her.

In the next few days, he did his best to dismantle the movement, but it had gained too much power. The King and gone into hiding. Fortunately, Cartella's forces beat the rebellious troops back, and he convinced the people that his decision had been wrong. The movement lost strength, and the muscles weakened.

The plan to take over the King's throne and annihilate his heir was stopped. The war became smaller and smaller, becoming nothing but a mere dent in the kingdoms, and the war that was supposed to happen never took place, much to Karl's' frustration.

He hated Victor, but he despised himself for not foreseeing it. Karl had never expected Victor to change his heart, and he had Isabella to blame for it. However, he rallied his soldiers, ensuring they still harbored their intense hatred toward the king.

His forces were not powerful enough since he had not stayed long enough with the Earthlings to greatly influence them. However, the king got wind of it and went into hiding, appointing Isabella as an acting authority.

Meanwhile, due to this move, Isabella and Cartella successfully managed to arrest many rogue rebels who had kept up the attack. They had stormed into the palace, but Victor had informed Cartella of the insurrection earlier, and she was waiting for them with her own forces.

A fierce battle ensued, generating casualties on both sides, but fortunately, it did not break out into a full-blown war. Cartella took a lot of prisoners and led them to the Palace dungeons. Victor had spilled everything to Cartella, so the King, his advisors, Isabella, and Aster all knew that

Everwell (Karl) was behind the attacks and he had been the one who had conspired it all.

Knowing his cover had been blown, Karl quickly fled.

However, Karl had suspected that his downfall might have come at the hands of the ones he'd trusted the most. When he fled, he dragged-Tatun and Rye's revolting minions with him, who had previously decided that Captain Karl deserved to be brought to justice.

Karl had fled in a panic without any of his weapons. Fortunately, his so-called minions had taken all the precautions necessary. They were equipped with Earthling weapons as well as traditional Hermes weapons.

'Maybe they were still loyal,' he thought. *'Thinking ahead was a good thing.'*

He didn't know then that his minions had utterly turned against him and had their own plans.

Karl, being in irrational escape mode at the time, coupled with his broken spirit, made it easier for them to overtake and restrain him and painstakingly drag him back to the King. He didn't see it coming. The ego had gotten in the way. His own holiness had blurred his foresight. All his plans of ruling the Earth had backfired.

"Why?" Karl shouted as he was dragged back to the kingdom through the moors. His voice echoed all around the large, open space. "Why have you betrayed me?"

"You have done enough!" Rye said dryly, forcing him onward.

"You will never be able to control the forces without me.

You will have to go back without ruling the Earth because you cannot." Karl screamed.

"Bold of you to assume we are like you," Tatun grimaced. "We do not wish to rule the Earth, Karl. We want peace?"

"How dare you call me Karl?" the Captain thundered, struggling against them but to no avail. "You're supposed to call me, sire. You are supposed to call me King. I am your captain. I can destroy you with the chips placed in your heads."

He reached down, only to see that his arm bracelet had been broken.

"We deactivated those," Rye said smugly, and then they both dragged him back to the dungeons and locked him up.

This, however, was not the worse betrayal.

Victor finally tracked Cartella down after her intimate confession to him and the kiss he could not stop thinking about. They had been working together, with him completely conforming to her notions.

He trusted her decisions since she was a strong, relentless woman with a dedicated work ethic. But when it became apparent that she was ghosting him, he started doubting their comradery. Desperately wanted to deny it, but still needed to know.

He kept trying to convince himself that he was not in love with her, but Victor had always loved Cartella since they were kids.

Once, while they played in the mud as five-year-olds

will do, he had drawn the two of them as stick figures standing beside each other and promised that he would marry her when he grew up. Eventually, he and forgotten his promise, and she did, too. But the kiss had ignited those memories and the feelings he had suppressed for so long.

He theorized that he was a womanizer and often lost in the overindulgence of cheap wine because of the suppressed feelings he had always held for her.

He missed the girl who had once been his best friend- the girl he had once been in love with, and Cartella's confession had opened up all those feelings again.

For some reason, even though he had tried to bring up the conversation, Cartella completely ignored it, turning away.

When he spotted her practicing in the weapons room, he entered and quickly bolted the door behind him so she couldn't escape, ignoring that she could easily outmaneuver any of his advances. He knew she was a highly skilled warrior, and for the first time in his life, he was willing to accept it.

"What do you want?" she spat, not looking at him, and her tone bothered him. She confessed to loving him, yet she still treated him coldly.

"We need to talk," he said, and she nodded.

Turning toward him, she said, "The rebellion has been halted. The people at the forefront are arrested, and I suspect it will die down in a few days. Additionally, Karl has been arrested, and he won't be creating any more problems. Good talk. Now I need to leave."

"What about the confession?' Victor asked.

"What confession?" she demanded.

"When you told me you love me," he reminded her.

"Oh, that," she said dryly. "Yeah. That was a lie."

She ducked under his arm to go out the door.

"A lie?" he asked, catching hold of her waist and stopping her.

She freed herself, and impatience coated her expression.

"Yes. I lied to get you on my side. I didn't expect you to be so gullible, but it worked," She said with a smirk, ready in case he decided to attack.

Victor, on the other hand, was utterly broken. Even if she had lied, his feelings had been completely genuine, and once he had stopped repressing them, they came back to him so strongly that he knew there was no way he could ignore them.

"Why?" he asked brokenly.

Cartella shrugged.

"Because I can," she said and exited, leaving him alone. He didn't go after her. His heart crumpled and folded like discarded trash. His dreams of being King added to the idea of having the love of his life beside him as his Queen, but all faded in a heartbeat.

How could she? It was his karma for thinking he should believe in a drifter such as Everwell. He should have known it was all too good to be true.

Through her sympathetic nature, Cartella had not exposed him entirely of his dishonest involvement.

'There may be hope yet,' he thought.

Thank God Victor was not a vengeful man.

In the interim, a new species, the Arrivals, had arrived. They were from the future and had seen the Earth's plight, so they returned to help.

These were from a planet called Iris, and they planned to save the world and prevent history from repeating itself. They were there to stop the subsequent great destruction.

CHAPTER 13

THE REVEAL

The new arrivals were time travelers from the planet Iris. Their primary purpose was that of peace since they had already witnessed the destruction that Earth received during the chaos the Pirates and Hermetites created while foolishly competing against each other for what Irisians called *'Ignorant- total- world- dominance.'*

Saffron, the leader of this small group of Irisians, stood on top of what appeared to be a simple levitating platform. Securely holding the handrails of the enormous craft that seemed to float over the land. Its ability to pivot quickly gave them the advantage of escape if needed in enemy pursuit since it was against their nature to stand and fight. The craft was large enough to transport armies but became obsolete with the new protocol on the home planet. They now used it to traverse over rough terrain staying close enough to the ground to avoid detection from afar. Its size was overkill for personal use, but Saffron liked it. They would sometimes pick up large objects like downed shuttle parts to analyze. The open platform allowed headroom for anything as long as it was tied down and secured. It looked like a flying white plate.

Her reddish blonde hair flew behind her, and her pale skin glimmered in the sunlight. She was lovely, but all of the Irisians were. They glowed with inner peace, which was understandable since they were harbingers of goodwill.

"What have we gotten so far, Ramon?" she asked, her voice like the chime of silver crystal bells. "What is the status?"

Ramon, the man beside her, draped his arm over her shoulder. He was her dominant lover but knew when to step down and assume his ranking position.

"So far, my love," he started. "Captain Karl is still in prison, but he is making his escape as we speak. The winter solstice draws closer, and the pirates are getting angsty. We have fifteen days to prevent the great destruction from happening."

"Only fifteen days to stop the war?" she asked with a deep sigh and then settled into his embrace. "So many interrupted timelines, so many tries and retries, and I still can't believe this is our last chance. If we fail to prevent the Hermetites' ship from self-destructing and blowing up the planet, this will all be for naught. Earth will die, and I fear it will take us with it this time."

"We can always go back home," Ramon suggested. "Where there is just the two of us, our small clan, and the little piece of heavenly happiness we found on Iris."

"You don't get it," Saffron said. "Our planet struggled so much before. I went through so much turmoil only to face destruction. I don't want that to happen to any other planet." It Seems Iris had gotten complacent at one time with their security procedures and let the wrong ones into their timeline, causing years of confrontation and devastation to many parts of their planet.

Ramon kissed her forehead. "I know, sweetheart. But Earth was doomed to fail. We can't play hero and save all civilizations. Some things must be, and sometimes the future, regardless of how many times we try to go back and change it, is set in stone. It is only by changing ourselves that we can change the circumstances around our future, and neither the Hermetites, Pirates, or Earthlings are capable of change. They seem to have destruction and potential for greed hardwired into their very veins."

"I know what you mean," Saffron said. She spun two fingers in the air, using the metal ring she wore on those two fingers to direct the floating Device back to their domain. It was a small, silvery ship with barely 20 people on board, and it could cancel a hundred percent of light, and practically all the colors of the rainbow, because it was covered with multiple small, light-canceling techno devices.

It could completely camouflage itself in plain sight simply by reflecting-a hundred percent of the light coming toward it. Saffron's tribe had been destroyed by the Pirates, but she had not sought them out for revenge. Instead, she had visited Earth to prevent the Pirates from doing the same again.

When they arrived on Earth, using the Irisian's

time-hopping skills, she discovered that the Hermetites, not the Pirates, would be the reason for Earth's second great apocalypse, and she refused to sit back and watch it play out again.

The Irisians were a peaceful tribe that supported universal peace and took active steps to ensure it happened. They had pale, almost shimmery skins, slender physiques, and gentle faces. In the following years, the proof of any existence of the Irisians would be distorted and expressed as Folklore in the latter cultures.

However, the Irisians were not earthly technological. Just like certain species had certain redeeming characteristics and particular traits specific to them, Irisians could bend around time and space matter, hopping from one timeline to the next, rendering them an advanced species, comparatively. They were from a place of no weapons, being much too involved in diplomacy over possessing power. Iris was a planet of serenity. It was not known by many since its appearance was usually cloaked. Word of mouth within the planetary system was only hearsay. Some travelers doubted their existence.

Iris was protected from Pirates and would be villains. The ones that did visit were allowed in by the upper council. Preparations had to be arranged to open the frequencies long enough to let a traveler in. They were well equipped to rule all the others but chose not to, mainly to maintain their status of serenity.

Iris was composed of a million different wavelengths of light, allowing them to manipulate numerous frequencies and the world of Iris. They had derived a method of using these frequencies, giving them invisibility and time travel so they decided to use their abilities for good and helpful acts to the less fortunate.

Saffron knew that some timelines were so warped that the outcome would remain unchanged regardless of how many things were changed. Some timeline's are uncompromising.

"I am just terrified, Ramon," she admitted.

"Terrified about what?"

"Maybe we are not the ones who can bring peace to this world. We have tried it before, and it did not work. Maybe for this planet, the future is set in stone," she confided.

"Ah, but remember enots nac eb dekcarc htiw retaw," he reminded her.

"Literally, stone can be cracked with water. So we only have to try. We have to be persistent to save the Earth. Isn't that what you want?"

"I do. But I also fear that we may end up ultimately destroying it. Our interruption and experimentation with this may ultimately alter the balance of a timeline. Earthlings have always been the specie to be feared the most. All the different species in the universe are either good, like us, or destructive, like the Pirates. Earthlings are the only species that have the potential to be both. They have deep reserves of compassion, and yet, they can also be terribly malicious, and that is why I am skeptical about interfering with their future," she said.

"Just say the word, and we can leave. We don't need to look back," Ramon assured her.

"I can't do that," she said, shaking her head gently. "Our future could depend on what happens this time. Timelines can only be altered so many times. This is our last chance. Send out one of our messengers to the warriors Cartella and Victor. We need to inform them about our arrival."

"Not the King? Not Aster?"

"No. This time, we will rely on the people who are much more mindful of the world around them. In another timeline, Aster is a villain, the king is a fool, and Cartella is in love with Victor. Let us see what this timeline brings us," she commented softly.

"And may it bring us peace," Ramon added as they entered their domain.

"Who are you?" Victor asked, looking at the handsome man standing before him.

It was the Hana, the Irisians' messenger. She had a shock of thick, dark hair and bright green eyes. Her glowing, translucent skin set her apart from the Earthling, but the Irisians was a specie that could take on the most aesthetically appealing form to the person looking at them.

The Earthlings may think of those abilities as "sorcery" or "magic," but there are always proper scientific explanations for everything. Irisians could appear aesthetically pleasing to humans because they could alter perceptions. Since Irisians could manipulate components of light, they could appear in a way that was aesthetically pleasing to whoever looked at them. That was also how they could pass off as "lovely strangers."

"I would like an audience with the warrior's Victor and Cartella. I have urgent news from my species," Hana said.

Echoing down the extended hallway that gave access the all the army barracks.

Victor fidgeted uncomfortably, uneasy with the alien interruption of the declassified meeting he was presiding over.

'Next time, I will be more discreet with my location,' Victor thought.

"You may talk to me. Cartella might not be willing to give you an audience. Now, what species did you say you were?" Victor demanded, running a scenario in his head of how he might have to quickly subdue this young alien.

"I am very willing to grant an audience," Cartella said, and Victor looked up.

His eyes caught hers, and he scowled, looking away, unsure when she had snuck up on them and how much she had heard.

Things between them were still awkward. He tried to be as casual as possible, but it was hard to shove his heartbreak to the side and keep living as usual. Dances, women, and drinks no longer interested him, especially after he discovered that Karl and Cartella had separately manipulated him into looking like a fool.

He wanted to always keep his head clear, and drinking

would only ruin his plans. He had no mood for revelry, given the seriousness of the situation,

"And as for women ..." his eyes caught Cartella's again.

'A certain someone has all my attention, and I don't think that will ever change,' he decided silently.

Hana nodded, and Cartella looked around, saying, "But it would be wise to have this conversation where prying ears may not hear us."

She snapped her fingers, and the soldiers immediately split apart, clearing her path. They were in the battleground, where the soldiers usually practiced daily. It was Victor's turn to head the practice, but she had come to check on his progress. She walked forward, Hana and Victor following close behind her, and led them to one of the inner rooms. There was no current Head of the King's Guard since Karl's treachery had been discovered, and the King had gone into hiding.

Isabella had instructed Cartella to take control of the forces, and she had quickly and successfully done so. The rebellion had been all but squashed, and her next mission was to restore peace to the kingdom so King Howard could finally step out from hiding.

'Hopefully,' she thought to herself. *'This alien showing up unannounced like this, doesn't create a roadblock altering my plans.'*

"Now, begin by telling me your name and species," she said calmly, not a semblance of fear in her voice. They were all alone, apart from Victor, and he had perched himself on a chaise lounge and was trying not to stare at Cartella.

"My name is Hana, and I am an Irisian from the planet Iris, but most of our specie has been killed off. We are beings of the light.

We lived in darkness and cold for centuries, losing loved ones with each season. Our lives can't end naturally, but our species can no longer reproduce," Hana explained.

"And what is your reason for being here?" Victor asked, having begun to pay attention to the conversation.

"The Hermetites and the Pirates want to destroy the Earth and control all of you. We want to try and save it by preventing all that from happening," Hana said. "And before you ask, we would benefit nothing from this. Our leader, Saffron, lost most of her tribe in the great destruction that overtook our planet long ago, and she has taken the role of saving the known universe and its all species upon herself."

Victor found it hard to wrap his head around the entire concept of it, because '*why would anyone help someone if they weren't getting anything out of it?*'

Cartella, however, had no problem accepting that this new species had possibly reached a different level of self-actualization and was working purely out of a sense of altruism. The Hermetites were based on logic and peace. The pirates' ideology was only based on war, and personal gain, the Earthlings could be good at both. The Irisians, on the other hand, had surpassed all personal desires and operated according to the benefit of others, which was known as 'pure altruism.'

"So kind of like, you're keeping us from going extinct?" Victor asked, and with a snort, Cartella had to prevent herself from giving in to the urge to laugh. Hana just looked confused.

"Never mind that," Cartella said quickly. "You said something about the Pirates. How could that be? The Pirates were killed out a while ago when Isabella...."

"Orchestrated the battle of the sea?" Hana finished the sentence for her and shook his head. "Not all. Some survived, and they repopulated. They are a threat to the Earthlings. As for Captain Karl, we have foresought that he is the one who will lead to the Earth's destruction. He is no Earthling. He is a Hermetite. He is their leader, the very man King Howard threw out of the Kindom when he first came to propose a faulty peace treaty."

Victor and Cartella exchanged a puzzled glance. The alien man already seemed to be aware of what was going on. That was not the only thing that shocked them, though. Neither of them had known that Karl was a Hermetite.

"Are you sure he's a Hermetite? Our king surely would not make such a mistake," Cartella said.

"Mistakes are made, even in Royalty," Hana quickly replied.

"At this very moment, the one called Everwell has already escaped his cell and is going through the moors. You may check if you please," Hana said, and Victor immediately bolted from his perch.

He called the guards into action and, within minutes, felt foolish after realizing that Everwell had escaped.

Mysteriously enough, the prison bars had been melted, leaving hardened molten puddles of steel on the ground.

This was unlike anything the earthlings were capable of. The guards had also discovered something they assumed was an alien metal melting stick left behind.

"He's telling the truth," Victor said, fixing Hana with a steely gaze.

Cartella turned back to Hana and said, "Okay. What do you want us to do?"

CHAPTER 14

BATTLE OF SHIPS

The deal was struck, even though there was no real deal to strike, and the Earthlings had begun an official collaboration with the Irisians. Saffron had yet to meet Cartella, but she was already planning to do so.

One thing was clear- the Hermetites were the true enemies, along with the Pirates.

Isabella, Victor, Cartella, Rye, and Tatun stood in the conference room. Tatun and Rye had proven themselves to be true warriors and, with ritual, assimilated with the Earthlings, living with them. Nobody knew they were Hermetites, just like nobody knew Aster's true identity.

Caretella placed one finger on the map they had spread on the table.

"According to the information Hana gave us, this is where the Pirates are, and this," she said, stabbing another area on the map with the tip of the dagger she held. "Is where the Hermetite ship is."

"But that is the sea," Victor said, glancing at the map. "How can it be under the sea? What are they? People with the ability to breathe underwater. The Brotherhood talked about this, but I thought it was just a joke!"

"That's where Hana said it was," Cartella told him.

"Exactly there?" Victor said. "We don't want to accidentally attack the wrong place only to find out it is some distance away."

"Actually," Rye said, stepping forward. "That is exactly where the ship is. Underwater. But since supplies on the ship are dwindling, it may rise over the water in a few days. Give it a few days. The Hermetites might make their way to shore soon, and when they do, we can take their ship."

"How do you know all this?" Isabella asked, always quick on the uptake.

"My brother and I have sources," Tatun said gravely.

"We get around," Rey intervened with a smirk of innocent defiance.

"And what if your so-called sources are wrong?" Victor demanded, causing a vocal ruckus of several opinions at once.

"Look!" Victor shouted over the roar. "It's not like we have any other options here. It's just waiting a few days. It won't hurt.

Meanwhile, we need to take down the Pirates. Isabella, do you have any ideas? You strategized the war against them the first time," Cartella piped up.

"We all know that the Pirate's main weakness is fire, so we can prepare for that, but know this, they can hide in the smallest of spaces. They do this to avoid the day's heat," Isabella said.

“How about this,” Victor said, his eyes brightening up. “We could use flame throwers. “It’s something Everwell spoke of in my presence once.” He was trying to sugarcoat his actual conversation. “He had inadvertently laid out plans for its construction. If I’m correct, it could remove the threat of the Pirates and irradicate them from all earth’s crevices.”

“How?” Cartella asked.

“Since fire repels the Pirates over our artillery, this should keep them at bay indefinitely. We can drive them back to where they came from simply because they will be too afraid to make any close-range attacks!” Victor said. “Convince them to eventually run back to their own home planet.”

Isabella looked at him with a new kind of appreciation

“A good place to start is with that device we found in Everwell’s jail cell. I’ll trust you to follow through with that, Victor,” she said.

“I’m on it. Victor proudly replied

“That- If we can harness that weapon, That’s brilliant,” she said, not noticing the smirk on Tatun’s lips. Tatun and Rey knew precisely what Victor was talking about.

He had already been discussing the flamethrower technology with Tatun and Rye when Hana interrupted him, and Cartella waltzed in and disrupted the meeting.

“And what about the Hermetites?” Cartella asked.

“They won’t come close. Most of their weapons are long-range and can only detect moving targets. They also have devices placed on our grounds. These blow up when stepped on," Rye said, making sure to not use any specific terms and keep the entire weapon concept simple.

"How do they work?" Isabella wondered. "I have never heard of something like that. They truly are advanced."

Victor suddenly jumped in with a scowling remark. "The question we should be asking is *'How did Rye know about these weapons?'*"

"That's not important at this time. How we get our information is insignificant. We now need to know if these Irisians have superior technology over the Hermetite's," Tatun said, quickly avoiding Victor's inquiry.

"Unfortunately, no," Isabella stated. "I asked Hana if he would be willing to provide us with any weapons, but he said their species believe in virtue. They do not produce or promote the use of weaponry."

"And you bought that?" Victor said in his pessimistic manner.

"The Hematites' weapons are long-range weapons that work by movement detection," Isabella continued.

"I've heard of those!" Rye replied. "Aster told me it's more of a heat detection than a movement. I had trouble understanding what he was trying to tell me at first, but now, as we talk, it's coming back to me. The slower you move, the less heat a body will secrete, making it harder for the armory to find its target. Moving slower would help, but we could wear garments to confine our heat. Only for cross-country marching, of course."

"Yeah, and later, cooling off in the river!" Victor suggested sarcastically.

"In addition, Isabella," Cartella remarked. "You told us they had buried exploding weapons that will kill foot soldiers when trodden on. Can they be detected and disarmed somehow?"

Isabella nodded and said, "Possibly. But there are no guarantees in war. Sending in animals to trod the area could be an option. Even though it is not natural to kill innocent creatures, it could help save soldiers. Let's avoid suspected areas like loose dirt and keep to the laid roads. It will leave us in the open and vulnerable, but it's the best I can offer you. We won't have the luxury of taking shortcuts for now, so make any tactical movements or relocations in the dark of night, when it's much easier to stay cool, and always remember to be on the alert while off-road. They are hard to see, so I'm told."

They all agreed, so Cartella decided to call it.

"Okay, the meeting is adjourned. Victor, you need to ensure the armory makes enough arrows to sustain flame tips, and Cartella, inform the troops what sort of weapons to expect. Also, Victor, look into that flame thrower. There must be others that know of it. Investigate what you can. I trust you with this. Team up with Cartella. She's the weapons expert," Isabella said.

They all nodded and made their way out of the hall.

'This could be my ticket to the throne,' Victor thought.

As Tatun and Rye had predicted, the Fortress rose out of the sea a few days later. Captain Karl walked across its docks, agitated by everything. He had contacted the Pirates and asked them for help. He knew that Tatun and Rye had betrayed him completely and were terrified that they would make use of the information he had given them.

At first, the pirate Tchaka was unwilling to provide the Captain with any support, but once Karl groveled and begged, the malicious Tchaka gave in.

He stood at the docks, watching Karl pace, and clutched the translation device the Hermetites had given him close to his gaping mouth.

"Why are we out of the sea?" Tchaka asked with a garbled voice due to an inferior translation mechanism. "Why ask us to bring our ship near to yours? I have my entire fleet on board. If you are planning something, remember that my men are always prepared for combat. I decided to help now because we have a mutual enemy with King Howard."

Captain Karl stopped pacing and tried not to scoff. He hated asking the Pirates for anything but was in dire straits. He had an army at his command, but since his exile from the palace, that was no longer an option. He had initially wanted Tatun to be at the helm of the army and fight his war while he stayed inside the ship and sipped some nectar.

Unfortunately, Tatun and Rye betrayed him at the wrong time. Just when they were needed.

Karl wanted to scream at Tchaka for being insufferably narcissistic, but he knew he had to control his temper to have the Pirate's continued support. He knew a new species from planet Iris had settled on Earth and had already collaborated with the Earthlings. He was unaware of the extent of the Irisians' power, but he knew he had to be careful.

He could not underestimate them.-Finding the Pirates' ships had been easy enough, but he did not know where the Irisians had landed their ship. He found no evidence of any vessel that had brought them there.

Even though he would never admit it, this terrified Karl.

"Karly, are you listening? Karly?" Tchaka asked, making Captain Karl wince while watching his men sparring with the pirates who had jumped ship on Karl's deck. They were so close to each other, and with a warring nature, the temptation for a true-blooded Pirate was too hard to resist.

He hated the nickname Tchaka used for him and would rather rip out his ears than have the disgusting translated voice say 'Karly' one more time.

"What?" he snapped at Tchaka.

"Your men are bothering my men. Look over to the ships," Tchaka pointed out. "Tell them to stop."

Karl looked over and saw that the Pirates had started attacking the Hermetite forces.

"What are they doing?" he wondered. "Why are they attacking?"

"So this is what your true plan was?" Tchaka growled, turning to Karl. "You wanted to get my forces to fight yours under the guise of an alliance against a common enemy!"

"No. I assure you that was not the plan. Something must have happened. I need to check up on my forces," Karl said calmly, but Tchaka was not someone who could be appeased, nor was he the kind of person who listened to reason.

Tchaka attacked Karl, but Karl dodged. Neither possessed weapons, so they had to use their physical strength, and Tchaka had a clear advantage.

"Stop fighting!" Karl called out to the men on his ship, but nobody noticed him. He dodged Tchaka's attacks, shouting to his men to stop, but to no avail.

"They attacked us first!" one of his soldiers shouted, and Karl realized what must have happened.

He turned to Tchaka, wide-eyed, and pointed a finger toward him.

"You planned this!" he yelled, and Tchaka grinned.

"Planned what?" the Pirate asked. "To pretend to be in alliance with you and then take you down while accusing you of doing the same thing?"

Karl slammed his fist toward Tchaka, who dodged, and then the Pirate swung out, hitting Karl on the jaw.

Burning pain spread through the area where Tchaka had hit him, and Karl blindly grabbed the item closest to him, flinging it in Tchaka's direction. He heard a clang of metal and a shout, which alerted him that he had hit his target.

Karl smiled, his grin bloody, and spat out a pointed tooth. Tchaka growled and shot toward him, grabbing Karl by the neck and trying to choke him, but Karl kicked out, and when that did not work, he brought his knee up and drove it into Tchaka's stomach, making the Pirate get off of him.

He quickly glanced away and noticed that his forces

were still fighting. In the distance, he saw something else, a sight that made his eyes widen, and he almost forgot about defending himself. Tchaka's punch caught him square in the diaphragm knocking the air out of him. He took a few steps back, coughing, still reeling from the hit, and held his hand up.

"Stop!" he yelled. "The Earthlings. They are coming. Stop!"

Tchaka, however, was not one to listen to reason. He had seen the Earthlings surround the shore, armed with some bow and arrow weaponry, but he didn't care. The Pirates had fast healing, and the only thing that could harm them was the fire. He struck another blow toward Karl, who dodged and kicked him in the gut.

"You don't understand. We need to unite," Karl said, but Tchaka growled a curse word, holding up a metal bar and slamming it on Karl's head.

Karl raised his hands to defend himself, but it was too late. He was knocked out cold. Immediately, Tchaka took the same metal pole and twisted it once and then twice, binding Karl's arms with it. He looked up and saw that his forces were on the verge of winning against the Hermetite forces.

"The self-destruct!" one of Karl's warriors shouted, but he was drowned out.

"We can press the self-destruct and kill them all!" he shouted again, standing behind a broken part of the ship's hull.

"Are you insane?" another Hermetite said. "That kind of

sonic power can't just destroy the ship. It can also destroy us in the process."

"Then I can die for honor," the first Hermetite said, sticking out his arm and shooting lasers at some of the Pirates. However, the Pirates were a terrible enemy to have.

"Honor has nothing to do with it. If we blow up the ship, we go with it, the Pirates and this entire planet go with it. It's just plain stupidity," the second Hermetite said.

"It's that strong?" the first one asked, and then the two of them were abruptly attacked by a horde of savage Pirates who fell upon them, biting and scratching at them.

Cartella, Victor, and the vast Earthling army stood at the shore, dipped their bows into alcohol, lit it with flames, readied themselves, and then shot toward the Fortress and the Pirates' ships. The arrows were to announce their presence. Their primary weapons, however, were the flame throwers that Rye and Tatun had helped them design.

The battle had officially begun.

CHAPTER 15

THE PARADOX

"The core reactor!" Karl shouted at his forces. "Self-destruct the ship!"

He struggled against his bonds, but the metal around his wrist was too tight.

"Self-destruct! Self-destruct! SELF-DESTRUCT!" he kept shouting, hoping that his fellow Hermetites would hear him and sighed in relief when they did.

"Stay silent!" Tchaka snarled with his best attempt at Earthling dialog. He grabbed another pole and tied Karl's feet together to prevent him from kicking out. Karl wriggled along the floor like a worm, and Tchaka laughed. He pulled Karl's head and smashed it into the side of the Fortress.

"Why are you doing this?" Karl pleaded. "We could have worked together. We still can!"

"You insult my pride. Together? Ha! We work alone, and we will rule alone. You will die," Tchaka roared.

Karl could comprehend most of what was being spewed from the mouth of the pirate, crude as it was, although the hand gestures he'd picked up from Garnish helped.

"Say whatever you want," Karl said, displaying a bloody grin. "You will die right alongside me."

"You're the one who's tied up," Tchaka pointed out. "And you are the one who is going to die."

The Earthlings had made their way forward. They had abandoned the arrows since they had been more of a signal to their reinforcements and had started making their way forward with flamethrowers in hand. Cartella and Victor were at their helm, leading the forces forward. Rye and Tatun had boarded the Pirates' ship, with the other Hermetites, in an attempt to slow the invasion.

The Pirates were driven back by the force of the flames. The 'cool-temperatured' Hermetites were also somewhat threatened by the flamethrowers but mostly confused.

Karl's first thought was, *'Have more Hermetites arrived with help?'*

But then saw Victor holding the fire and-wondered how it had fallen into Earthling's hands.

'How did the Earthlings harness their own technology in weaponry?' Karl wondered.

As more Earthlings started boarding the ships, beating back both Pirates and Hermetites alike. They certainly weren't taking the time to evaluate who was the more significant threat. Since the battle was spontaneous, originally meant to be a peaceful meeting, Karl and his men were unprepared. Their only defense was the weapons they consistently carried.

The core reactor, which powered the main engine,

was exposed during the chaos. Rye made his way toward Cartella.

"The reactor!" he shouted at her. "We can't let any weapons or the flamethrowers hit the reactor. It will cause an explosion that will destroy the entire world!"

Cartella looked at him, her heart sinking in dread.

"But how can we stop our forces? They aren't even following my orders. It has gotten completely out of control!" Cartella roared over the noise of the battle.

"You can do it, Cartella! It's what you do best. I'll go to the engine room and see if I can shut them down," Rye pleaded desperately.

Cartella nodded.

"Okay," she said. She caught sight of Victor and approached him, but he was too preoccupied with the battle to notice.

"Victor!" she shouted. "Victor! Turn them back. Make sure they don't get close to the reactor."

He didn't hear her and just flashed her a bloodthirsty grin. She scoffed and went down the corridor, intending to stand guard. Just as she reached it, there was a flash of light in the sky.

The Irisians had arrived.

They had some small, translucent, and spherical devices that seemed like the sort of glittery object a child would play with. Still, when thrown from their floatation platform, it hit the ship's surface and exploded, demanding everyone's attention.

Cartella watched, mesmerized, and realized they were

approaching the reactor. She had to stop them. Three Hermetites attacked her, and she started fighting them off, trying to move them away from the reactor. She slayed one of them with her sword, but the others kept fighting. They had lost their weapons somewhere along the way and picked up the Earthling's weapons instead.

Victor drew closer to her, intending to join in the fight, but before he could reach her, a Pirate advanced up beside Cartella and shoved a dagger-like knife into her stomach.

"No!" Victor yelled, but Cartella kept fighting. She seemed unaffected. She decapitated the Pirate, throwing him overboard, and then looked up at the sky, where the Irisians had thrown another of their spheres.

"No!" she shouted. "No!"

The ship stopped shuddering under her, the vibrations dying down completely.

BOOM!

The device hit the reactor, and then there was a loud sound as it exploded. Rubble and metal flew everywhere, and Cartella was flung against the ship's far side near Victor. She braced herself for the impact, and when it came, it was worse than expected. She coughed up blood and tried to take deep breaths, already feeling the life quickly drain out of her.

She had expected the reactor to react, she thought she and the rest of the world would die, but then she saw Tatun emerge from the side of the boat, accompanied by Rye and realized that they had done it. They had deactivated the engine before it could self-destruct. That was what had probably killed the vibrations.

The world didn't end!

She wanted to cheer, but another groan came out of her throat. Victor made his way beside her and panicked and cursed, but when he saw her look up at him, he had a relieved grin.

Cartella was dying, and she could feel it, but at least the rest of her warriors were safe. She smiled at the thought.

"No! No, no, no. Why are you smiling?" Victor roared at her, abandoning the battle, leaning down, and trying to stop the bleeding. The force of the impact had left two of her legs wholly disfigured and burnt, and countless pieces of shrapnel had pierced her, but he would not let her die.

He refused to let the woman he loved die.

"It's fine!" Cartella said, looking up. "This needed to happen."

She closed her eyes, and Victor grabbed her shoulders and gently shook her, trying to keep her conscious and alive.

"You won't even let me die in peace?" she snapped through frail lips. But Victor was persistent. He held her to the end.

Tears flowed down Victor's cheeks, but then Cartella smiled. She coughed and mock-glared at him before beginning to close her eyes. No amount of nudging or coercing made her open them again, and her heartbeat slowly faded. He knew she was gone once he felt her last breath touch his cheek.

Meanwhile, the Irisian's stood on the deck of their ship, watching Tchaka torture Karl.

"Leave him to us," Saffron demanded, and Tchaka stiffened, knowing that this new species had too much power to mess with. Still, he was not one to back off.

"No. I kill him. He is my kill," Tchaka insisted.

Ramon stepped forward and looked at Saffron, who nodded. In one fluid movement, Ramon jabbed two fingers into the space on Tchaka's body where his Pirate heart existed, causing him to fall, instantly dead. Ramon opened his hand, exposed the small shocking device that had stopped Tchaka's heart, and suddenly withdrew from the battle.

Then he bent down and held Karl by the neck, dangling him a few inches off the ground so Saffron could look at him.

"Captain Karl of the Hermetites," Saffron spoke. "You have caused so much destruction. And for what?"

"You're one to talk," Karl scoffed. "If someone hadn't deactivated the engines to the Fortress, your shiny device would have destroyed the Earth when the ship self-destructed."

Saffron ignored him.

To her, Karl was filthier than the grime under her shoes. She disliked him for many reasons, but mainly for his conniving, selfish ways. Earth was not the only planet he had tried to destroy under the guise of *'keeping peace in the universe.'*

He was a selfish man who had tried all he could to

dominate as many planets as possible. That unjustly earned him his title as a captain, but it had also been the deciding factor that made Saffron recognize him for the scum he was.

"So what?" Karl asked. "You're going to kill me?"

"Oh no. Killing would be too merciful. Where you are going is a terrible place you won't escape from. Ha-Mun-Ra!" she said.

"Ha-Mun-Ra?" Karl laughed. "That's only a myth."

Ha-Mun-Ra was a place where evil people were condemned to a diabolical existence, and once entered, any resemblance to reality was removed from the convict's notion. It was a space where evil gathered. Not exactly a black hole, but a time termination, where each person who entered was stuck in a horrifying time loop that would eventually drive them insane, which was not too far from where Karl already was.

'Amusing,' Saffron thought. *'He should fit in nicely there.'*

Moreover, since each person was stuck in one of the infinite loops, most were alone forever. They could not age, and they could not die. Nor could they escape. Eventually, the loneliness drove them to an empty, desolate state of mind removing all internal emotions.

"You will never hear another voice for all of eternity. You will possess nothing but a blank stare wandering around in the space of your own fears. A fitting punishment for one as wicked as you," Saffron declared.

The Irisians had kept the loop and its secrets for ages, but it had been temporarily disabled when their planet was destroyed in their own wars. Once Saffron had found its entrance again, she had learned to open it at will.

She then appeared to be in concentration, twisted her hands in a circle, and opened a portal in front of them. Ramon grabbed Karl, forcibly throwing him into the opening. Terrified, he screamed as he fell. Then she suddenly closed the portal and looked around.

The battle had started to move inward toward the human cities.

"We can't stop these forces. We need some weapons," Ramon said.

"The bell," Saffron replied. "The bell in the middle of the cityies. The Earthlings use it to call for attention, but in the last timeline, it was a device that could terminate any beings that weren't Earthlings. We should remain unaffected because we are only remnants of light but all Hermetites and Pirates will be wiped out."

"But how do we activate it?" Ramon asked.

"Isabella and Aster," Saffron reminded him. "Aster's parents designed the bell. He knows how, and Isabella is one of us, is she not?"

"Isabella is an Irisian?" Ramon demanded. "I thought she was human. She always played a human role in the other timelines!"

Saffron grinned.

"That is because she longs to be one. She lives these human timelines as often as we reset them because her affairs are always human, and she so cherishes those relationships," she told Ramon. "We simply reverse her energy into matter to give her the substance to coexist."

They jumped back on their platform and headed toward the bell. Isabella was already waiting for them and standing near the bell. Aster was a little distance behind her.

"Another timeline?" she asked, with a small sigh. "Let's end this. There is not one version where Earth will be safe. This is how it is, time and again."

"We must try our best to make all planets prosper, Isabella. As long as there is hope, we will keep trying because we advocate peace," Saffron told her kindly.

"Sometimes peace needs sacrifices!" Isabella said. "Maybe the world would be more at peace without the Earthlings. And without all of us. We have tampered with too many timelines. It is time to stop. You are tinkering with time and seeking out forbidden timelines."

"Forbidden?" Saffron demanded. "All we want is peace."

"No," Isabella said wisely, shaking her head. "You do not want peace. You want to be labeled as the *universe's 'harbinger of peace.'* You want the title."

"That is not true," Saffron said, stepping back.

"It is!" Isabella insisted. "Let's stop. Let this war end. There is no need to protect the Earthlings. They can protect themselves against others. Let this be."

"Your lover?" Saffron said, her eyes lighting up. "What about him? Are you willing to never see him again?"

"I'll see him after I die," Isabella said.

"We Irisians don't die. We have eternal life spans," Saffron scoffed.

"But we can be killed. We are as susceptible to weaponry as any other species. And when I am killed, I will rejoin my lover," Isabella pointed out.

"That's impossible. You don't even know what comes after death. Nobody in the universe does!" Saffron shouted.

"Perhaps I don't," Isabella replied. "But I am willing to find out."

Saffron gestured to Ramon, and he immediately restrained Isabella. She could quickly subdue him, but she didn't find any reason to do so. She stayed content, completely calm. She had lived too long to be flustered by anything.

"You don't know what the bell does in this timeline," Isabella said.

"In the previous timelines, it wiped away everyone who didn't have Earthling blood, including the animals, and us, Irisians," Saffron quipped.

"It didn't wipe away Aster," Isabella pointed out.

"That's because his parents designed it to recognize him!" Saffron snapped before turning to Aster.

"Now," she said. "Operate this."

Aster looked at Isabella, who just shrugged, letting them do whatever they pleased. She hoped they would learn their lesson in time.

Slowly, Aster made his way toward the bell. His parents, who had been Hermetites rebels, had designed it to kill any species that dared to attack the Earth or Earthlings. They knew Hermetites forces would come after them, and they needed something to protect themselves after being banished. That was why they had created the bell.

As tradition went, it had been rung by Earthlings in time of need, but it had always indeed been a weapon.

With trembling fingers, Aster slowly slid his fingers across the carvings on the bell, tracing the small circles to activate them. When fully traced anti-clockwise six times, the three inscribed rings on the sides of the bell started to glow. Aster traced them once more, then went to the rope and pulled it once.

The world stilled, and then it was no more. A blinding light spread from the center of the bell and enveloped everything. Earth did not explode. It simply broke into smaller atoms as if it had never existed in the first place.

The Irisians were the species that had set out to save the world, but in that specific timeline, the bell had not been a form of protection against foreign species. It had been a destruction device. It destroyed the world and everyone in it, and there was no chance for recovery.

The sun spun along on its axis, and the rest of the planets continued to revolve, but Earth's axis was empty.

The paradox of trying to save the world ultimately resulted in its destruction, and that was what happened.

Or did it?

Because timelines are tricky things, and things are never as hopeless as they seem.

EPILOGUE

"I'm just glad we were able to board this ship," Darius said as he and Settii crouched behind a large object that looked like a large furnace.

It produced heat, making it comfortable, and warded off the cold. They didn't know, nor did they care, where they might end up, as long as it was off this nightmarish planet.

"I'm glad too, Darius. We're a good team," Settii said softly.

The ship was large enough to conceal their presence for a while, as long as they kept alert and were stealthy to survive on the minimal food scraps they had previously committed to ration during their trip.

The decision to leave their home planet was a challenge, although having the only home they knew and loved-destroyed right before their eyes helped make that decision for them.

Over time, their patriotism toward their planet had dulled, and the destruction of the beauty of nature had left them with so much despair that they had no other alternative but to escape and pray for the best.

“Who would have thought it would all come to this?” Settii said dismally.

“There is nothing left to break, aside from our spirit!” Darius added. “They’ve destroyed everything.”

“They’ll never break me!” Settii exclaimed.

Spaceships were not something either boy was familiar with. They had curiously wandered within the belly of the metallic ship, which looked so much bigger from inside. It had arrived just before the war ended. Destruction had taken its toll on the landscape. The traditional Eaeth architectural foundations had crumbled under the more potent forces, and their army was too weak to sustain the protection needed.

Originally, the Irisians had been determined to disembody the planet, but the boys were the first to befriend the newcomers when they arrived and showed them the compassion that was thought to be nonexistent, changing their intent. They had agreed to chauffeur Saffron and Ramon, showing them the destruction of monumental castles, homes, and villages. Settii even advised them to move on, and take them with them.

It was the only option left to them. The opportunity to leave their planet had been non-existent until now.

The boys’ advice fell on deaf ears. The new arrivals saw a cursed world and didn’t want to bring that curse upon themselves.

They weren’t interested in offerings, or suggestions, for that matter. Their agenda was different.

They could move through time, but to do so they needed

fuel. To be more specific [Radiation] is freely available in the depths of space, but limited on some planets.

It seemed that Earth allowed a certain amount of radiation within its atmosphere, but radiation could be harnessed, much more easily through the opening of the planet's protective blanket called the ozone in the northern hemisphere.

Saffron pulled stakes and disappeared into the darkness that hid them as quickly as they had arrived. The sudden launch shook the boys to the point of panic.

'This is it!' Darius thought as he held on to the anchor bar used to secure cargo.

Settii sat on the floor.

'I will remain totally unbiased for the remainder of my life, however long that might be,' he thought.

He felt guilty for initiating the fighting when he and Settii intervened at the palace years ago.

'That was when it all seemed to change,' he mused. *'At the palace.'*

The ship's floor was cold but clean. Its vacant loading dock echoed their footsteps. Once they lifted off, they thought it would be clear sailing.

They thought that they would, at the very least, be away from the existing danger that loomed at ground level. The fighting had gotten so bad that everyone was an enemy.

Brother drew blade against brother, and families fought against families. Sides were pledged, and stubbornness prevailed. It was being told as a war to end all wars. Had they not escaped, they would probably be living in isolation or resorting to the original underground lifestyle the Pirates had led. It was unknown to both the boys what had just occurred at the Bell.

No sooner had the flight begun than it was over. The interior temperature of the ship had dropped so rapidly that it scared the stowaways into thinking they had made a horrible mistake. They could actually see their breath.

They were not prepared for the sudden climate change.

"What have we done!" Settii exclaimed in a whisper.

"We will surely die here!" Darius replied.

Suddenly two Irisians appeared from out of nowhere and boarded a shuttle. The Northern cold was not a problem for the Irisians since they were already accustomed to frigid climates.

The reason for the new arrivals' flight to the pole was not something the boy's could have predicted. They would have had no concept of inter-planet techno abilities. Believing that the ship had taken them to another planet, the boys instantly retreated back to the warmth of the engine and waited to see what the crew would do.

"We snuck onto a transporter, Settii! This ship is not leaving. It's only relocating," Darius panicked.

"You mean we're still at home?"

"We couldn't have traveled far in that amount of time. Maybe they're refueling," Darius suggested, trying to calm himself.

"But why is it so cold? Maybe they need the cold to help them fly?"

"Let me think on that," Darius said. By then, the word

(Planet) was a household norm, and most earthlings accepted the idea, but it was still a little beyond their conceptual understanding.

Settii nodded slowly. A few crew members suddenly came in, boarded a small pod, and quickly exited the loading doors, seeming to be in a hurry.

Both of them huddled behind an engine. They stayed warm enough until the crew finally finished their undertaking and lifted off again. This time, the ship made its way above the atmosphere.

Settii's stomach turned, and he felt nauseous from the free-spinning feeling and floating. All sense of direction had momentarily upended.

It seemed as if they never stopped going up. Through a small circular port hole, they could trade off watching to see their planet getting smaller until it exploded and vanished. The ship stopped vibrating, and a stillness overtook them.

'Very unnerving,' Settii thought.

Eventually, somehow above the hum of the engines, their adrenalin slowly letting them relax, they both fell asleep.

Awakening to the change of sound, they could also feel the ship slowing.

Looking through the port hole,

"Darius! Is that Earth? Are we landing?!"

"I don't know. I've never seen Earth like this."

Then just as suddenly as it had taken off, the giant ship came to a halt, hovering over land. They hid behind the engine housing and watched some crew members prepare to disembark. They were loading themselves into small pods and activating the internal mechanism that seemed to be some power unit.

It produced a low humming sound and emitted welcoming heat.

"Listen, Darius, we should probably conceal ourselves a while longer until we know a little more.

"I agree, It's never wise to jump into things."

After some time had passed, just as the boys started to get antsy, suddenly the ship started moving slowly towards the planet. Again, they experienced a lack of gravity for the first few minutes.

Peeping out of a service port, they saw something completely different from where they had left behind. It did not resemble their home and consisted of green vegetation, rivers, and roads. When they were even closer, they started seeing buildings.

'Where are we?'

"We've done it, Settii. We have arrived at a New World. It's beautiful!" Darius exclaimed. "It's Wonderful!"

Printed in the United States
by Baker & Taylor Publisher Services